THE HATE TRAIL

THE HATE TRAIL

Bradford Scott

GUNSMOKE

First published in the US by Pyramid Books

This hardback edition 2012
by AudioGO Ltd
by arrangement with
Golden West Literary Agency

ISBN 978 1 445 82392 8

British Library Cataloguing in Publication Data available.

Printed and bound in Great Britain by
MPG Books Group Limited

ONE

Flying lead plays no favorites.

Ranger Walt Slade, he whom the *peons* of the Rio Grande River villages named *El Halcón*—The Hawk—ducked instinctively as the slug sang past overhead.

The second one came closer, fanning his face with its lethal breath. A third twitched at the sleeve of his shirt like an urgent hand.

That was enough! He whirled Shadow, his tall black horse on a dime and skalleyhooted into a convenient alley. He was turning his mount to face the main street when half a dozen riders stormed past, shooting back over their shoulders.

A shotgun let go with a thundering roar. One of the riders yelped a curse. Evidently a pellet from the double load of buckshot had nicked him. But he stayed in the hull and kept going.

The shotgun cut loose with another blast. A couple of six-guns chimed in blithely. Down the street charged a gray-mustached old jigger with a big nickel badge pinned to his shirt front and the still smoking sawed-off in his hand.

"And don't come back!" he bawled after the retreating horsemen as they whisked around a corner and out of sight.

Glancing about, he saw Slade sitting his horse in the alley mouth.

"And where the devil did *you* come from?" he barked.

"I don't ask you where you come from, though I think I'd have a right to after you singeing my whiskers with your blue whistlers," Slade retorted. "What's the idea, anyhow? Can't a peaceable stranger ride into town without having to dodge hot lead?"

"You may be peaceable, but this blankety-blank-blank town sure ain't," the sheriff growled.

Glancing up the street, Slade felt that the remark was

5

something in the nature of an understatement. Two men, cursing and limping, were being helped along the board sidewalk. A third was swabbing his bullet gashed cheek with a bloody handkerchief. A fourth cherished a blood-dripping hand.

The sheriff continued to regard Slade with scant favor, a scowl on his bad-tempered old face. Slade smiled, the flashing white smile of *El Halcón*, that men, and women, found irresistible. The sheriff tried to glower, but instead he grinned, a trifle crustily, perhaps, but he grinned.

"What you want here, son?" he asked in somewhat mollified tones.

"First," Slade answered, "a place for my horse to put on the nosebag and take it easy for a spell."

"Turn him around and you'll come to a livery stable a hop and a skip down the alley," the sheriff replied.

"Then a place where I can tie onto a surrounding, and somewhere to sleep," Slade added.

"The Trail End saloon right across the street puts out a good surrounding of chuck, that is, if the kitchen ain't shot up too much—a notion it ain't."

"What started the corpse-and-cartridge session?" Slade asked.

"Hanged if I know for sure," the sheriff answered. "Those hellions who sifted sand out of town started it, I think. I ain't got the lowdown from anybody yet. And in such rukuses, everybody always blames everybody else—'I was plumb innocent, Sheriff. Was just mindin' my own business when that sidewinder cut down on me. Why? Hanged if I know.' That's what I'll get when I start asking questions. Did you get a good look at the hellions?" Slade shook his head.

"I'd just dived into the alley and hadn't got my cayuse turned around yet," he replied. "Didn't see their faces at all except a sideways glimpse as they turned in their hulls to shoot back."

" 'Bout the same with me," grunted the sheriff. "Well, they're gone and I expect they won't come back. Nobody cashed in, I gather, just a few punctures Doc Beard will take care of."

He hesitated, studied Slade a moment. "You asked about a place to pound your ear, I believe," he remarked. "Well, I won't rec'mend the fleabags they call hotels or rooming houses, but I've a notion Clint Adams—he runs the livery

6

stable—will have a vacant room over his stalls right now; he sleeps there. Tell Clint Sheriff Carter sent you and I've a notion he'll take you in."

"Thank you," Slade answered. "That helps a lot. I like to sleep close to my horse."

"So I expect," the sheriff conceded dryly. "Be seeing you. I'll amble over to the Trail End and see if I can learn anything—be darned surprised if I do."

Before the sheriff was half way across the street, he demanded querulously, of himself, "Now who the blankety-blank is *he*? Just comes to me that while I figured on trying to learn a mite about him, I did all the talking and he didn't say a darn thing."

Which, had the sheriff known it, was a peculiarity that had puzzled and bewildered wiser men than himself. Walt Slade would talk freely and pleasantly, almost volubly at times; but he wouldn't tell you anything.

Left to his own devices, Slade located the stable without difficulty. A husky individual with a blocky face and a truculent eye opened the door in answer to his knock. He gave Slade a glance, stared at Shadow.

"Bring him in! Bring him in!" he rumbled. Slade dismounted and did so.

"It's okay, Shadow," he said. The big black, who had flattened his ears when the keeper reached for the bridle iron, pricked them forward again.

"One-man horse, eh?" grunted that worthy. "That's the right kind. He'll get proper care, and be here when you want him."

"Sheriff Carter said you might have a sleeping room for rent," Slade observed. The keeper nodded.

"Brian Carter's all right, but the horse is a better rec'mendation," he said. "Yep, I've got a room open. First one at the head of the stairs; I sleep in the second. Key's in the door, and here's one to the front door. I don't often give 'em out, but a feller who rides that horse must be okay."

"Thank you," Slade said as he accepted the key and picked up his saddle pouches and rifle.

"Don't thank me, thank the horse," Clint grunted.

"I have, more than once," Slade smiled. "If it wasn't for him, several times over, I wouldn't be alive today."

"Don't doubt that," Clint said, running a keen glance over the Ranger's face and form.

He saw a tall man, more than six feet, with a breadth of shoulder that matched his height and a deep chest slimming down to a sinewy waist. Doubtless he found the sternly handsome countenance of his guest also arresting. The lines of a rather wide mouth relieved somewhat the tinge of fierceness evinced by the prominent hawk nose above and the powerful chin and jaw beneath.

The lean, deeply bronzed face was dominated by long, black-lashed eyes of very pale gray, cold, reckless eyes that nevertheless always seemed to have little devils of laughter dancing in their clear depths. But old Clint, a shrewd observer, felt that should occasion warrant, those devils, leaping to the fore, would be anything but laughing. His pushed-back J.B. revealed thick, crisp hair so black a blue shadow seemed to lie upon it.

Slade wore the homely but efficient garb of the rangeland with careless grace—bibless overalls tucked into well scuffed half-boots of softly tanned leather, a blue shirt with a vivid neckerchief looped at the throat. The broad-brimmed hat completed the costume.

Circling his waist were double cartridge belts, from the carefully worked and oiled cut-out holsters of which protruded the plain black butts of heavy guns.

And from those gun butts his slender, powerful hands seemed never far away.

"Trough of running water in the back if you'd care to splash the dust off," said Clint as Slade descended the stairs after stowing his gear in the plainly furnished but clean little room. "It's cold, but fresh. Soap on the shelf and a towel hanging on a nail."

"Thanks," Slade accepted gratefully. "That'll help a lot."

The sluice in the icy water was refreshing. After which he donned his well-worn garments, decided he could do another day without a shave and sallied forth in quest of the Trail End and something to eat.

"Now who the devil is he?" Clint asked of the unresponsive Shadow as the door closed on Slade's broad back. "Looks like a chuck-line-ridin' cowhand, but I'll bet my bottom peso he ain't. Oh, well, we're getting all sorts hereabouts of late

8

and I reckon one more won't hurt. I'm putting a snort in your water—goes well with oats. Don't do it for everybody, but you and him both are a mite out of the ordinary."

TWO

THE TRAIL END proved to be a typical cowtown saloon, bigger and better appointed than most. There was a long bar, a dance floor with a small raised platform to accommodate the orchestra, poker tables, two roulette wheels, a faro bank, a lunch counter, and tables for more leisurely diners.

Although it was still only midafternoon, the bar was well crowded, mostly with cowhands, and everybody appeared to be excitedly discussing the recent gunplay.

Sitting at a nearby table putting away a surrounding was Sheriff Brian Carter. He intercepted Slade's glance and beckoned.

"Sit down there where I can keep an eye on you," he ordered as Slade drew near. "Where'd you say you came from?"

"I didn't," Slade replied, accepting the vacant chair, "but if you're real anxious to know, I rode in from the west."

"So!" the sheriff exclaimed. "Got chased outa Oldham County and decided to give Potter a whirl, eh?"

"Well, the sheriff over there did think it might be a good idea for me to move on," Slade replied smilingly. He refrained from mentioning that the sheriff of Oldham County was an old friend who thought that Slade's "reason" for being in the section might possibly be hanging around Amarillo.

"I don't doubt it! I don't doubt it!" Sheriff Carter agreed heartily. "That hellion over there is always sending me trouble." He beckoned a waiter.

"Fatten him up so he can't slip between the bars," he directed.

"I'll do that, Sheriff," the grinning waiter promised, adding *sotto voce, but* not too *sotto* to Slade, "Try and get him to lock you up, feller. We send over the meals for the prisoners and fellers have been knowed to spit on the sidewalk just for a chance at getting free helpin's from the Trail End."

"You'll get a chance at some free helpin's if you don't keep your thumb outa my bowl of soup!" the sheriff declared. The waiter chuckled, took Slade's order and hurried to the kitchen.

"Learn any more about who started the shindig and why?" Slade asked. The sheriff shook his head.

"Best I can gather, somebody made a misdeal," he replied. "Those six hellions came in here together. A couple of 'em got in a poker game. There was a row and the other four, who were at the bar, joined in. I ain't sure just which side really started it. Card players are usually close-mouthed and you can't get 'em to talk. Prefer to settle their differences themselves."

Slade nodded thoughtfully. He wished he had gotten a look at the six riders who hightailed out of town.

"Aiming to coil your twine here?" the sheriff asked suddenly.

"Maybe, if you'll promise not to throw me in the calaboose just for the fun of doing it," Slade answered, with a smile.

"I ain't promising," said the sheriff. "Every stranger who ambles in of late either ends up there or ought to. It is a good section for cowhands, though. The spreads hereabouts are always short of help."

Slade knew that the shrewd old peace officer, despite the persiflage in which he indulged, was covertly studying him and doing a bit of probing. Well, one couldn't blame him. The Cowboy Capital was a trouble spot. There was no town organization and the affairs and laws of the community were administered by the county officials and it was up to them to try and keep something resembling order. Which was no easy chore and it was not unnatural that all strangers were to an extent suspect.

Slade's meal arrived and there followed a period of busy silence. Finally the sheriff pushed back his empty plate with a sigh of contentment. He hauled out a black pipe and stuffed it with tobacco. When the steamer was going to his satisfaction, he spoke—

"So John Davenport sent you over here, eh? Why?"

Slade regarded him for a moment. He liked the old fellow's looks, felt that he was trustworthy, not exactly stupid and could keep a tight latigo on his jaw. He decided to take him into his confidence, to an extent.

"Sheriff," he said, "did you ever hear of Veck Sosna?"

The sheriff's eyes widened. "Why, I reckon I have," he admitted. "He was the pack leader of the Comachero outlaws who raised heck in the Canadian River Valley and up around the Oklahoma Border a few years back. Yep, I heard of him; I was a deputy in those days. Why?"

"Because," Slade replied, "I have reason to believe that Sosna has returned to his old stamping grounds and has organized a following—he's a genius at that."

The sheriff jumped in his chair. "The devil you say!" he sputtered. "As if I didn't have enough on my hands! I—" his voice died away and he stared at Slade. Then he glanced around, leaned forward and lowered his voice.

"I've got you placed at last!" he said. "Been trying to figure it since I first clapped eyes on you. Now I've got it. You're *El Halcón!*"

"Been called that," Slade admitted composedly.

The sheriff gave a hollow groan. "*Trouble, trouble, trouble!*" he lamented. "Why'd you have to come here? Everybody knows trouble just follows you around."

"Perhaps you'll have less by the time I'm ready to leave," Slade replied.

"That's plumb sure for certain," the sheriff declared, with fervor. "Yes, sir, sure as the sun rising in the morning. And you're looking for Sosna?"

"Well, I've chased him all over Texas and Mexico," Slade said. "Thought a couple of times I'd gotten rid of him for good, but he's got more lives than a cat and has always managed to survive."

"Uh-huh, I've heard of the feud between you two hellions," growled the sheriff. "Maybe you'll finish each other off," he added hopefully.

"I hope you're wrong about that," Slade smiled. "I'd sure hate to have to keep on chasing Veck Sosna through eternity."

Sheriff Carter chuckled. "Reckon you must feel sort of that way about it," he conceded. "But mavericking around as *El Halcón*, an owlhoot too smart to get caught, will end up getting you in trouble. Oh, I know there are no reward notices out for you—I've heard that discussed—but give a dog a bad name—"

"First you have to drop a loop on the dog," Slade smiled.

"Oh, you're too darn smart for me to arg'fy with," snorted the sheriff. "But about Sosna, you really think he might show up here in Amarillo?"

"I've been wondering if he hasn't already shown up," Slade answered.

"Now what the devil do you mean by that?" demanded Carter.

"Nothing much, except I wish I'd gotten a good look at those hellions you chased out of town," Slade said. "Somehow it seemed to me that antic had the Sosna touch; I just can't help wondering a mite."

Sheriff Carter tugged his mustache and frowned. Abruptly he stood up.

"You stay right here," he said. "I'm going to mosey around and see if I can learn anything." He stalked to the bar and engaged the head bartender in conversation. Slade relaxed comfortably in his chair and rolled another cigarette. Things appeared to be working out rather better than he had hoped for. And that once again his *El Halcón* reputation was going to pay off. The sheriff, no doubt, considered him the lesser of two evils and would be glad to pit *El Halcón*, "the singingest man in the whole Southwest, with the fastest gunhand," against the devilish Sosna whose name was a byword throughout the Texas Panhandle country for ruthlessness, devilish ingenuity and sadistic cruelty. And, as the sheriff said, if the hellions did for each other, well—

Not that he really believed the old peace officer was that callous where human life was concerned. Just a subconscious assumption that in such an event his troubles would be lessened.

Due to his habit of working under cover whenever possible and often not revealing his Ranger connections, Walt Slade had built up a peculiar dual reputation. Those who knew the truth insisted vigorously that he was not only the most fearless but the most capable of the Rangers. Others, who knew him only as *El Halcón*, were wont to declare just as vigorously that he was just a blasted owlhoot too smart to get caught but who would get his comeuppance sooner or later.

Captain Jim McNelty, the famous Commander of the Border Battalion of the Texas Rangers, knew well that the deception laid Slade open to grave personal danger at the hands of some triggernervous marshal or deputy, to say nothing of professional gunslingers out to get a reputation by downing the notorious *El Halcón* and not above shooting in the back as a means to their end.

But he was forced to admit that the deception paid off at times, that outlaws, doubtless believing they had but one of their own brand and a lone wolf seeking to horn in on somebody else's good thing to deal with would at times grow careless, to Slade's advantage. Also that avenues of information were open to him that would have been closed to a known Ranger. So Captain Jim would growl and fuss but not actually forbid his lieutenant and ace man to continue the deception, allowing Slade to go his own cheerful way with little thought for the danger involved and with confidence in the future.

Among those who did *not* know the truth, Slade had champions as well as detractors. "Sure he's cashed in a lot of hellions, but just show me one that didn't have a killing long overdue. That's a chore for the sheriffs and marshals, you say? Huh! it's a chore for any decent and law-abiding citizen. More power to him!"

And the Mexican peons would say, "*El Halcón!* the friend of the lowly, of all who are wronged or sorrow or are oppressed. *El Halcón*, who walks in the shadow of God's hand!"

And Walt Slade felt he could presume to no higher accolade than that.

Sheriff Carter circulated for some time before returning to the table. Drawing up his chair, he beckoned a waiter and ordered a couple of snorts.

"Well, I think I learned something," he said. "Seems those six jiggers came in and lined up at the bar. Civil spoken and quiet and looked to be well behaved. After a bit a couple of them started watching a poker game and were invited to sit in. There were a couple of tinhorns in that game who've been hanging around here for a spell, and I've a notion one of 'em did pull something off-color. Anyhow, a row started and guns began to smoke. Swivel-eye Sanders, the owner, told me that one of the men at the bar, a big, tall and broad jigger with bright black eyes, did most of the shooting. Swivel-eye said he never saw such gun handling. Said it looked like to him that the big feller didn't shoot to kill, just to cripple."

"A wounded man can kick up more confusion than a dead one," Slade interpolated. "And throw more folks off balance."

"Guess that's right," the sheriff agreed. "Well, Swivel-eye said the big feller let out a beller and all six headed for the door, shooting over their shoulders. Guess everybody was too busy ducking to shoot back much. Out they went and piled onto their bronks, still shooting back over their shoulders. I got here just about then and cut loose with my scattergun, but the range was over-great for a sawed-off and I reckon I didn't do much good. Those two tinhorns, incidentally, after Doc Beard patched 'em up, they didn't come back here. Which makes me think they really did do a little chore of cold-deckin'. They picked the wrong crowd to try and slide one over on. What do you think?"

"I think," Slade replied slowly, "that it really was Sosna and some of his bunch; that shooting only to wound sounds like a bit of the Sosna quick thinking—he always seems to do the right thing. Did Swivel-eye or anybody mention what the others of the bunch looked like?"

"Uh-huh, the bartender said they struck him as having Indian blood."

Slade nodded. "Some of the Comancheros, I've a notion," he said. "Most all of them have a dash of Comanche."

"And the Comanches are the toughest and smartest of the Texas Indians," growled the sheriff. "Mean Indian and mean white! What a combination!"

"Yes, they seem to have inherited all the vices and none of the virtues of both races," Slade commented. Suddenly a thought struck him.

"I believe you mentioned the big fellow shouting an order," he remarked.

"Uh-huh, Swivel-eye said he let out a beller," the sheriff nodded.

"Call Swivel-eye over," Slade suggested. "I'd like to ask him a question or two."

Carter stood up, caught the owner's attention and beckoned.

Sanders, big and bony and burly, lumbered over to the table and Slade realized how he came by his peculiar nickname. His eyes were quite remarkable. One eyelid hung continually lower than the other, thus lending to his otherwise rather saturnine face an air of droll and unexpected waggery.

14

He seemed to glower with one eye and leer jocosely with the other. But he had a good nose and his mouth was well shaped. Slade figured him to be okay.

"This gent would like to ask you a question, Swivel," said the sheriff.

"Shoot," replied Swivel, one eye regarding Slade seriously, the other with whimsical humor.

"Mr. Sanders," Slade said, "I believe you mentioned to Sheriff Carter that you heard the tall member of the bunch who started the trouble here shouting an order to the others. Do you recall anything peculiar about his voice?"

"Yes, I did," Swivel-eye conceded. "Sorta unusual voice— sounded like it had bells in it."

"Thank you," Slade said and did not comment further.

"I'll send over a snort," said Swivel-eye and headed back to the far end of the bar.

"Well?" the sheriff asked, gazing curiously at *El Halcón*.

"It was Sosna, all right," Slade said. "He has the kind of a voice that once you hear you never forget. Swivel-eye described it quite aptly when he said it sounded like it had bells in it. It does have bell tones. Yes, as I said before, that antic, if it's the right word for it, had the Sosna touch."

Just about that time, had the sheriff and Slade known it, another "antic" was building up that most certainly had the Sosna touch.

THREE

A STAGE COACH ran from Tascosa to Amarillo—Tascosa, the former "Cowboy Capital of the Plains," before the hoped-for railroad bypassed it. A dying town that before many years would be little more than a memory.

But Tascosa wasn't dead yet, quite a ways from it, and its shops and saloons still did plenty of business. In consequence, the stage often packed quite a considerable sum of money in a locked strongbox, bound for an Amarillo bank.

With the Canadian Valley, a terrain favorable to the depredations of outlaws, crossed without mishap, and Amarillo not many miles ahead, the stage rolled along blithely, approaching one of the few stands of thick chaparral, with occasional trees, that flanked the trail. Beyond the chaparral was the open, treeless prairie.

On the high seat, an alert guard sat beside the driver, shotgun across his knees. A rifle leaned against the driver's knee. Both were conscious of the strongbox inside the locked coach; there were no passengers today, but that strongbox packed a hefty sum of dinero. Now, however, nearing Amarillo as they were, guard and driver relaxed a bit, conversing animatedly, their subject the anticipated night in town.

The stage entered the chaparral belt and a few minutes later careened around a bend.

"Look out, Prate!" the guard shouted.

The driver hauled back hard on the reins. Directly in front, the motionless body of a man lay face-downward across the middle of the trail. Nearby stood a saddled and bridled horse that gazed at the prostrate form and held up one foreleg.

The stage jolted to a halt, the prancing lead horses almost on top of the body. Overhead a tree arched its heavy branches and thick foliage across the trail.

"Cayuse has a busted leg—must have fallen and pitched the jigger on his head!" the guard exclaimed excitedly. "Looks like his neck's busted. I'll—" he glanced up as a slight rustling sounded over his head. An instant too late.

From the screen of leaves overhead whisked two tight loops. They encircled the shoulders of guard and driver and were instantly jerked taut. The unfortunate pair were snaked from the seat, shotgun and rifle clattering to the ground, and hung yelling and cursing and kicking, but helpless.

From the encroaching growth bulged three masked men. The "dead man" in the trail leaped erect and also proved to be masked.

"Stop your blasted kicking and be still if you don't want to stay still forever," boomed the taller of the group. The double click of a cocking gun emphasized the order.

The driver and the guard hung rigid, hardly daring to breathe, swaying gently back and forth like spiders on a web-

16

thread. Two more masked men slid down the tree trunk, chuckling and casting derisive glances at the hogtied pair.

A couple of shots smashed the stage's door lock. The strongbox was hauled out. A couple more shots opened it, revealing packets of bills and rolls of gold coin.

Two of the robbers dashed into the brush to return a few moments later with saddled and bridled horses. The money was transferred to saddle pouches. The "dead man" cut the thin cord that had held up his horse's front hoof to simulate a broken leg. All six mounted and turned their horses west.

The tall leader lingered a moment, gazing speculatively at the shivering guard and driver and fingering his cocked gun. Then he uncocked and holstered the iron.

"Hang aound for a while, gents, and enjoy the scenery," he said with sardonic humor and galloped after his companions.

It took the furious pair some little time to free themselves and drop to the ground. They retrieved their fallen arms, climbed onto the seat and, raving and cursing, sent their rifled vehicles roaring to Amarillo.

Slade and the sheriff were still sitting in the Trail End, discussing cups of steaming coffee, when the driver and guard stormed in and business came to a standstill.

"The blankety-blank-blanks!" howled the driver. The guard mouthed incoherent profanity.

"What the devil's the matter with you two?" shouted the sheriff. "What's wrong—what happened?"

The story came out, vividly spiced with cuss words. Sheriff Carter outswore them both.

"Did you ever hear tell of such a pair of terrapin-brains?" he demanded of Slade, after he had caught his breath.

"An old trick, but it works," the Ranger replied. He turned the full force of his cold gray eyes on the excited pair and they fell silent.

"How far from Amarillo were you when it happened?" he asked.

"Just a few miles," replied Prate, the driver. "Took us less than half an hour to get here; we came fast."

"But not fast enough so far as you're concerned, I'd say," Slade remarked to the sheriff. "If they headed west, they're in Oldham County by now, the chances are. So I guess

17

you'd better wire ahead and send word to Sheriff Davenport telling him what happened and to be on the lookout for the hellions. Not that it's likely to do him much good; chances are they'll slide into the Canadian Valley and make for a hole-up somewhere. Sosna knows the Valley like the palm of his hand."

"I'm sure hoping for a chance to get my hands on *him*," growled the sheriff. "It happened in my bailwick."

"Maybe you will," Slade comforted him.

"Any notion how much they got?" he asked the driver.

"I don't know, but I figure it was plenty," Prate replied.

"Shipment to the bank here?"

"That's right."

"Better notify the bank officials, too, without delay," Slade said to Carter.

"I will," replied the sheriff. "Come along with me?"

"If you wish me to," Slade agreed, rising to his feet.

"Take care of you later, Swivel," the sheriff said. They left the saloon together.

"Say, who is that big feller?" asked Prate, the driver, as he accepted a drink. "He seemed to take charge of things right off, told Carter what to do and everything."

"Don't you know?" asked Swivel, glowering with one eye and leering with the other. "That's *El Halcón,* the outlaw."

"Huh!"

"That's right," said Swivel. "The notorious *El Halcón.* Looks like a hawk, don't he? Like one of those big gray mountain devils that'll give an eagle his comeuppance. Yep, name sorta fits him."

"But how come him and Sheriff Carter are so chummy, if he's an outlaw?" demanded Prate.

"Oh, Slade—that's his name, Walt Slade—always takes sheriffs in tow," Swivel explained airily. "Reckon they figure it's best to have him close so they can keep an eye on him."

Outside the saloon the sheriff paused, glancing questioningly at Slade.

"Telegraph office first," the Ranger decided. "Then we'll visit the bank president or cashier and notify them of what happened."

The message for Sheriff Davenport of Oldham County was sent.

18

"May be an answer," Slade said to the operator. "If so, hold it for the sheriff."

Next they repaired to the home of the bank president, on Pierce Street. That official did a very good job of swearing himself, for a bank president, when informed of what had happened.

"The so-and-so's made a good haul," he growled. "I can't say as to the exact amount, but there must have been something between thirty and forty thousand dollars in that box, judging from what's usually sent to us."

"Insured?" Slade asked. The banker nodded.

"We won't lose anything, but it'll hit the express company hard," he said. "Up will go their premiums. Maybe the insurance people will drop them and they'll have trouble getting another to take them on. What you going to do about it, Carter?"

"I'm hanged if I know, Bob," the sheriff replied wearily. "It happened in Potter County, but Slade here is of the opinion that by now they are over in Oldham County and perhaps down in the Canadian Valley."

The banker shot Slade a shrewd glance. "That's the way you figure it, eh?" he asked.

"I'm not committing myself absolutely," the Ranger replied quietly. "I merely voiced an opinion, a little while ago."

"Hmmm!" said the bank president. "And you might possibly change your opinion?"

"Not beyond the realm of possibility," Slade conceded. Another shrewd glance from the banker, but when he spoke it was to the sheriff.

"Got a notion it wouldn't be a bad idea to listen to him, Brian," he said. "Got a notion."

The sheriff nodded but did not further commit himself one way or the other.

Outside the banker's residence the sheriff, though not a jovial soul, gave vent to a loud chuckle.

"I was just thinking," he said, "that here the sheriff of the county is taking advice from *El Halcón*, the notorious owlhoot."

"Well, there's an old saying," Slade returned, " 'Set a thief to catch a thief.' "

Sheriff Carter chuckled again. "You may have something there, son," he admitted. "Well, got anything to suggest?"

"I have," Slade replied. "That is, if you're willing to follow a hunch that has very little on which to base it other than what I've learned from experience, some of it not pleasant, just how Veck Sosna is liable to operate."

"I'll follow anything that promises results," the sheriff replied. "Right now I'm on something of a spot, and there's an election coming up this fall. Bob Evans, the banker, ain't feeling very good about this business and he packs considerable influence. Let's hear what you have to say."

Slade answered with a question. "How many deputies have you?"

"Three, all good men."

"Can you round them up in a hurry?"

The sheriff nodded.

"Three with you and I will be enough," Slade said. "Get hold of them and we'll ride west; you can swear me in as a special, if you care to."

"West?" repeated the sheriff.

"That's right, on the chance that the hellions will turn and head back this way, which I'm of a notion they're doing just about now."

"You mean to say you think they might come back to Amarillo?" the sheriff demanded incredulously.

"Why not?" Slade countered. "Their faces were not seen. Neither the driver nor the guard could identify them. They'd be perfectly safe in Amarillo, so far as they know."

"How about the row they kicked up in the Trail End?" said the sheriff. "They'd be recognized as doing that, all right. Why couldn't I throw them in the calaboose for disturbing the peace?"

"What row they kicked up in the Trail End?" Slade answered. "I listened to the talk at the bar. Everybody was pretty well agreed that those two tinhorn gamblers started the row. You can be sure *they* are not going to sign a complaint. With everybody confident that they pulled a little chore of cold decking, they'll be out of sight for a while. You can sometimes get by with a killing, but not with an engineered misdeal. They know it. You'd just get yourself laughed at. Sosna knows that and is not in the least worried about trouble being made for him because of that little rukus in which nobody was

20

cashed in and the possible complaining witnesses not present. But there *is* another angle. . . ."

"What?" asked Carter.

"Just this," Slade replied. "I don't think that Sosna knows I'm in this section. Otherwise, knowing I am quite conversant with his methods, he'd very likely not try it. As it is, I figure it's just the very thing he's likely to do. It would relieve him and his bunch from possible suspicion; nobody would suspect a bunch of stage robbers would be so brazen as to show up here in town in but a few hours after pulling a holdup. And that's just the way Sosna works."

"Dadgum it! you've sold me a notion against my better judgment," the sheriff said querulously. "How the devil did you do it?"

Slade laughed, and did not explain.

During the course of the conversation they had been walking to the sheriff's office. A light burned within and they found the three deputies whiling away the time at cards. They stared at the man whose exploits, even though some of them might be regarded as questionable, were the talk of the Southwest, when Sheriff Carter performed the introductions.

Briefly, Carter explained what he had in mind. "It's Slade's idea," he concluded, adding gravely, but with a twinkle in his eye, "He don't like for other owlhoots to horn in."

"I can understand that," observed Deputy Bill Harley, a lanky individual whose leathery countenance was as impassive as a green hide. "Johnny Davenport gets ringey when you start working on his side of the county line. A feller should stay in his own bailwick. Live and let live is the right notion."

"Get the rigs on your bronks, and come loaded for bear," ordered the sheriff. "We're going up against a salty bunch."

"And if we do come up with them, be ready to shoot fast and shoot straight," Slade interpolated. "They're desperate men and I doubt if they'll surrender without a fight. I don't know about the others, but Sosna is a dead shot. Very likely the others are also handy with their irons. We can't afford to take chances."

The deputies nodded soberly and hurried out. Ten minutes later the posse was riding west at a fast pace.

There was a nearly full moon in the sky, that was cloudless, and the prairie was flooded with silver light, which worked well with Slade's plan. For he had a definite objective in view

21

and believed he would be able to attain it—the belt of chaparral where the holdup occurred. He reasoned, knowing how Sosna's mind worked, that the outlaw leader would have been in no hurry to ride east. Better to let things cool down a mite before approaching Amarillo, then slip into town unobtrusively. He felt that the last thing Sosna would expect was a posse riding from the east after the driver and guard told of him riding west. Which was doubtless his reason for allowing the pair to live; Sosna usually left no witnesses.

All of which the Ranger had carefully considered before urging Sheriff Carter to head west with his posse on the chance of intercepting the outlaw band. He believed his hunch was a straight one and that there was a good chance to put an end to Veck Sosna's career of robbery and murder once for all.

Not that he was sure—he'd had too much experience with the Comanchero leader's uncanny ability to wriggle out of what appeared to be a tight loop. His hairtrigger mind plus his perfect coordination of brain and body had enabled him to more than a few times escape from what seemed an absolutely hopeless situation. Veck Sosna was a formidable opponent for even *El Halcón*.

El Halcón versus Veck Sosna! A saga of the West that would be talked about for many a year.

Suddenly the sheriff exclaimed, a trifle apprehensively, "Suppose'n we just run into a bunch of cowhands coming to town for a bust? Starting a corpse-and-cartridge session with them would be a fine howdy-do."

"Law-abiding citizens don't get trigger-nervous when called upon to halt by a peace officer who announced himself," Slade pointed out. "You don't need to worry on that score."

"Guess that's right," Carter agreed, in relieved tones.

Slade himself was doing a mite of worrying. He felt confident that he had sized up the situation correctly and that they had plenty of time to reach the belt of chaparral before Sosna. But suppose he had guessed wrong and the outlaws would get there first and from its shadow spot the posse riding blithely across the moon drenched prairie? Sosna's quick mind would instantly understand and react accordingly. The thought made Slade feel a bit cold along his backbone.

Finally they sighted the chaparral belt, which was very

22

broad to the north, running almost to the downward plunge of the wild Canadian River Valley. Slade instinctively slowed the pace a little and his eyes probed the shadows ahead.

It was an uneasy business, riding into what might well be a sudden blaze of gunfire. A blaze they would see but not necessarily hear, lead travelling somewhat faster than sound. His right hand hovered close to his gun butt as they drew near the dark and silent growth.

It was with a sigh of relief that, riding slightly ahead, he reached the stand of growth without anything happening. Again he slowed the pace.

"Easy now," he told his companions. "We want to find a good spot to hole up and wait."

He led the way until they came to where a tall tree stretched its branches across the trail, effectually shutting out the moonlight for the space of a dozen yards or so. Directly ahead, some twenty paces distant, the trail curved. The moonlight poured down on the bend and the straight-away beyond the tree. Slade pulled to a halt.

"This'll do," he said. "We will be in the shadow and they'll be in the light when they round the trail, that is if we don't have to wait too long; the moon moves and soon the whole trail will be in the shadow. I've a notion that right here is where the holdup occurred, from the description Prate, the driver, gave of it."

"Figure you're right," said the sheriff. "Okay, boys, just take it easy till the ball opens, if it does."

A tedious wait followed and Slade grew acutely uneasy. The moon was drifting steadily westward and already the edge of the trail at the bend was growing shadowy. A little more of that west by slightly south trend and their advantage would be wiped out.

A few more minutes passed, then the Ranger stiffened to attention; his keen ears had caught a sound that steadily grew louder—the soft drumming of hoofs on the dusty trail.

"Get set!" he whispered. "They're coming. Crowd your horses against the brush. Carter, you do the talking. You're a peace officer and you'll have to give them a chance to surrender."

"The hellions don't deserve it, if it's really them," the sheriff breathed. "Can't take a chance, though, it might *not* be them."

23

A couple of minutes crawled past. Then around the bend, clearly outlined in the moonlight, surged a group of horsemen, six in number. Slade instantly recognized the tall, broad-shouldered rider slightly in front. It was Veck Sosna! The sheriff's voice rang out—

"In the name of the law! Elevate! You're covered!"

The riders jerked to a halt with startled exclamations. Instantly Veck Sosna acted. He whirled his horse and sent it charging into the growth to the north. Slade drew and shot, but knew he had missed, for even as he pulled trigger, Sosna crashed into the brush and out of sight. And for the moment Slade had his hands full.

As if their leader's move had triggered them, his followers went for their guns. The growth jumped and quivered to a roar of sixshooters.

Slade shot left and right, and again. He saw a man topple from his saddle. A second slid sideways to the ground. Lead stormed all about him, one slug graining the flesh of his right arm, another ripping the shoulder of his shirt. His companions were shooting as fast as they could pull trigger, but the light was uncertain, the horses rearing and plunging. One of the deputies gave a yelp of pain. Another barked a curse. His horse, gone half loco, charged in front of Slade and he had to hold his fire.

The three remaining outlaws whirled their horses and, one slumping forward in the hull but keeping his seat, sent them careening back around the bend, the posse yelling and shooting in pursuit.

FOUR

WALT SLADE did not join the pursuit. Instead, he sent Shadow worming his way through the growth to the north, on the faint chance that he might overtake Sosna. It was not impossible that the uncanny hellion had figured what he

24

would do and was holed up somewhere waiting for him. To the devil with him! He'd risk it.

In fact, seething with anger, he was in a mood for anything. Once again Sosna had given him the slip when he thought he was all set to drop his loop. The sidewinder wasn't human!

Of course Sosna always had one advantage. Slade could not shoot him on sight. The stern code of the Rangers held that the quarry must be given the chance to surrender, and Sosna was not restricted by a code of any kind. He *would* shoot on sight. The devil with him!

Slade rode on, Shadow avoiding as many thorns and low-hanging branches as possible and plainly disgusted with the whole futile performance. After what seemed a long time they reached the final fringe of the brush. And less than a half mile ahead was the lip of the Canadian River Valley.

There was nobody in sight. The prairie lay silent and deserted in the white flood of the moonlight. As disgusted as his mount, Slade turned west and rode until he had skirted the belt of chaparral. Reaching the trail he pulled up, and rolled and lighted a cigarette. In the far distance to the west he could see rising and falling blobs that were doubtless the posse. Hooking one long leg over the saddle horn, he drew in deep drafts of the satisfying smoke and waited. His normally cheerful disposition was regaining the ascendancy. Sosna got away, his luck plus his uncanny ability still held. Oh, well, maybe next time! He watched the sheriff and deputies draw near and waved a reassuring hand.

The posse straggled to where he sat, their horses still breathing heavily.

"Any luck?" called the sheriff. Slade shook his head.

"Hellion got away," he replied. "Oh, it was Sosna, all right; I recognized him first off. How about you?"

"No luck, either," growled Carter. "The sidewinders had better cayuses than we did and pulled away in a hurry, edging toward the Valley. When they went over the edge we gave up. I think one was hit—rode like he was. Anyhow, I figure we did for a couple of 'em. Let's go see."

When they reached the bend in the trail, the sheriff's judgment was vindicated. Two dead men lay in the dust, their horses nosing about and trying to graze on the scanty grass fringing the edge of the brush.

"Ornery looking specimens," Carter growled as he dismounted. "Indian blood, all right. Let's see what they got on them."

"First, is anybody badly hurt?" Slade asked.

"Oh, Perley has a slice along his arm and Wayne a hunk of meat knocked outa his gunhand, nothing to bother about," the sheriff replied. "I tied 'em up and they'll do till Doc Beard gets a look at them."

While the sheriff and the deputies were going through the pockets of the dead outlaws, unearthing odds and ends of no significance and quite a bit of money, Slade approached the horses and opened one of the saddle pouches—each rig boasted two. He rummaged about inside, drew out a shirt and a pair of overalls. Then he hit paydirt. His hand came out filled with packets of bills of large denomination and a couple of rolls of gold coin.

The other pouches produced more treasure. "Looks like they divided up before they turned back east," he observed, passing the money to the sheriff.

"Say!" exclaimed Carter, "we didn't do so bad. With what they had in their pockets, must be eight or ten thousand dollars here; we'll count it carefully when we get to the office. Packing in a couple of carcasses and all this dinero ain't bad at all."

"But the he-wolf of the pack made it in the clear," Slade observed morosely.

"He'll get his, sooner or later, on that I'm willing to lay a hatful of pesos," the sheriff predicted cheerfully. "Hoist 'em up, boys, and rope 'em to the saddles. Good looking cayuses, too. We'll turn 'em over to somebody who can use 'em. All set? Let's go; I'm hungry."

The cavalcade got under way, the bodies jerking and flopping grotesquely to the motion of the led horses. Everybody was cheerful, the sheriff and the deputies chattering away blithely. Slade had recovered from his moment of depression and joined in the talk from time to time. Might have been worse. At least he had given Sosna something of a jolt, and right now the outlaw leader wasn't feeling at all too good over the night's happenings. Slade doubted that he realized, just yet, that *El Halcón* was again on his trail and was probably puzzling his head as to how he had been outsmarted.

Not that he would pay much mind to the loss of two of his followers—he could get more—and very likely he had tied onto the biggest share of the bank loot. But being outsmarted was something else again. Outsmarted and lured into a trap. That wouldn't set at all well with Veck Sosna.

Well, as Slade had learned through experience, if he got mad enough he was also prone to get a bit reckless, which Slade considered was to his advantage, especially if Sosna had not yet learned he was in the section. He rode on in a complacent frame of mind.

Although it was past midnight when the posse arrived in Amarillo with the fruits of victory, there were still plenty of people on the streets. People who stared in astonishment at the grim procession and converged on the sheriff's office.

Soon the deputies were circulating through the crowd, explaining, answering questions. Admiring glances were cast at Slade. The sheriff was complimented and congratulated on the success of the venture.

The bodies were laid out on the floor and covered with blankets. Several citizens and a couple of bartenders were convinced they had seen the unsavory pair in town quite recently.

With the recovered money safely in the office safe and the wounded men packed off to the doctor, Sheriff Carter shooed out the crowd and locked the door. After which he and Slade and the uninjured deputy, sardonic Bill Harley, adjourned to the Trail End and something to eat.

In the saloon they received more congratulations and the details of the episode had to be repeated. Slade let Carter and the deputy do the talking, and found Harley's dry humor refreshing.

After finishing his meal he smoked a cigarette and announced, "I'm going to bed. See you in the morning, Sheriff. Suppose there'll be an inquest?"

"Oh, I reckon Doc Beard will want to set on 'em," Carter replied.

"He's county coroner and figures he should do something to earn his pay. I've a notion he'll be a busy man from now on, and so will the undertaker, if you run true to form. Take care of yourself, son, be seeing you."

As was his habit, Slade approached the livery stable warily. Everything was peaceful, however, and after cleaning and oiling his guns he went to bed and slept soundly until mid-morning.

After a sluice in the trough and a shave, he repaired to the Trail End for some breakfast. Next he dropped in at the sheriff's office and learned that the inquest wouldn't be held until two o'clock. With time on his hands, he decided to look the town over a bit.

In the three years since Slade had visited Amarillo, the new Cowboy Capital had grown more than a little. It was indeed a far cry from the original railroad construction camp that was its inception. In the beginning it was a collection of buffalo-hide huts that served as a supply depot and shipping point for the hunters, then sweeping the last of the great buffalo herds from the prairies. It boasted a hotel, the walls, partitions and roof made of buffalo hides. When dry, the hides became to a degree transparent; so there were not many secrets in Ragtown, as the settlement was called.

The passing of the buffaloes did not much affect the little community sprawled beside the railroad tracks. Some gentlemen of thrift and vision realized the commerical value of the buffalo bones bleaching on the prairies, and bone gathering became a thriving industry, to the emolument of Ragtown, for many thousands of tons of bones were shipped for fertilizer within the next few years.

Then along came the great cattle ranches and Ragtown sat up and took notice. Also taking notice was another gentleman of vision, a land developer named Henry B. Sanborn. Mr. Sanborn, looking to the future, was confident that here was the natural site for a town that one day would become the metropolis of the prairie empire known as the Texas Panhandle. In which Mr. Sanborn was right.

So Mr. Sanborn laid out a town site southeast of Ragtown, at a point where the railroad tracks curved around a natural body of water called Amarillo Lake. He called his town Oneida. There had been a protracted dry spell which greatly reduced the water area. Mr. Sanborn made a mistake when he began erecting his buildings, railroad station and stockyards. Everything was going nicely when along came the rains, and they kept coming. Before long the incensed Mr. Sanborn saw his buildings, railroad station and stockyards standing in four feet of water.

Mr. Sanborn was a man who put up with no nonsense. He went away from there, taking his buildings and stockyards with him to higher ground, their present location, where they

28

would be safe from the clutches of pestiferous Amarillo Lake. He left the name "Oneida" behind and changed the name of his town to Amarillo, perhaps as a taunt to the now frustrated lake. Very quickly, Amarillo swallowed up Ragtown and suffered pangs of indigestion thereby.

Mr. Sanborn, amongst many other merits, had that of being an adroit politician. He wanted the county seat of Potter County for his town and proceeded to get it. As it happened, the cowhands of the great XL Ranch constituted the majority of the legal voting strength. Mr. Sanborn offered the cowboys a town lot each if they would vote for his town for county seat.

The cowboys, proud to become land owners, did so, and victory for Mr. Sanborn was easy. Some of the waddies who were the recipients of the real estate were smart enough to hold onto their lots, to lease but never sell. As a reward for their perspicacity, they in later years became wealthy.

So when Walt Slade strolled along Filmore Street that sunny morning, Amarillo was on its way, but with still some distance to go. Cattle had supplanted the buffalo as the horned kings of the prairie, and the great ranchowners were the "feudal lords" of the Panhandle.

Not that their sovereignty was unchallenged. Already the plow was moving westward, bringing with it that abomination of the oldtimers—barbed wire. Both were and would be productive of trouble.

Yes, Amarillo was on its way, but was still as wild a frontier town as one could hope to find. Lines of cow ponies stood tied to the hitch racks of the main streets, and their riders crowded the hotels, saloons, gambling houses, dance halls and restaurants. Teamsters, railroad workers, and gentlemen of doubtful antecedents did their gentle best to keep things lively, and succeeded. Food consisted largely of canned goods, beef, and wild game. A pile of empty and rusting tin cans marked the rear of every eating place as conspicuously as the sign in front. The "sovereign seal" of the Panhandle might well have been crossed skillets with grease dripping.

At the moment, however, Walt Slade was more concerned with Amarillo's present than Amarillo's possible future. He knew that the town was the lodestone for the lawless elements of the section, their favorite spot when in search of diversion.

Here they came to drink and carouse, and when the redeye began getting in its licks there was always the chance of somebody doing some loose talking.

Such a character as Veck Sosna could hardly operate in the section without attracting the attention of the local chapter of the share-the-wealth brotherhood. He was very likely a prime topic of discussion at owlhoot *conversaziones*. So Slade hoped that he might catch a word here or there that would provide a lead which would give him a line on his elusive quarry.

With which in mind he dropped into several of the less reputable saloons, toyed with a drink and listened to all that was said within earshot. But as two o'clock drew near he had not so far heard anything he considered of significance. Finally he gave up for the time being and headed for the sheriff's office with the inquest in mind.

FIVE

THE INQUEST didn't take long. The coroner's jury 'lowed that the two horned toads got just what was coming to them and a similar treatment for the rest of the bunch as quickly as possible was recommended. Everybody who took part in the venture was congratulated. Doc Beard banged his gavel and adjourned the proceedings, observing that he hoped for a repeat performance in short order.

"And now what?" asked the sheriff when they reached his office and sat down.

"Now," Slade replied, "I'll be beating my brains out trying to figure what Sosna will do next. No doubt but he is furious over what happened last night and will be out to even up the score. Somebody is going to catch it."

He paused to roll and light a cigarette and after the brain tablet was going good continued:

"My chore is to try and anticipate his move and, if possible,

30

thwart it. We were lucky this time to get off without loss of life—Sosna doesn't usually leave witnesses, and with him in the temper he now is it's very likely that his streak of sadistic cruelty will come to the fore. I'd say his only reason for letting the driver and guard remain alive yesterday was his desire that they report him and his bunch heading west. Next time will very likely be different."

"The snake-blooded devil!" growled Carter.

"Sometimes," Slade observed, "I find myself actually wondering if he is a man and not really a devil. One thing is sure for certain, he is a madman. Yes, a mad genius who somehow took the wrong fork in the trail. He is an educated man, a graduate, *summa cum laude,* from a great university. He could write both M.D. and Ph. D. after his name if he chose to do so. He thinks and acts with bewildering speed, witness last night, when he instantly took the only course by which he could hope to save his hide. He was into the brush almost before you spoke."

"He's a heller, all right," agreed the sheriff. "How'd you come to get tangled up with the sidewinder?"

"It's quite a story," Slade replied.

"I'd like to hear it," Carter said.

"Okay, here goes," Slade answered. "I first contacted him in Tascosa. He tried to kidnap a girl there—dealing in women sold to the Indians or the New Mexico outlaws was one of his operations. I frustrated his attempt and nicked him in the arm, which didn't set well with him. So he tried to kill me a couple of times, which didn't set well with me."

"That I can understand," chuckled the sheriff. Slade nodded.

"Then I managed to spoil a raid or two for him. After which I trailed him to the Cap Rock hills and by way of the 'Trail of Tears' to the hidden valley where the Comanche Indians used to take their women and children captives. With the help of some poor devils he was holding there as slaves, I smashed his bunch. But Sosna escaped. I followed him through the hills to the open prairie and thought I had him in my loop. But at the last minute, when I was closing in on him, a freight train had to come along. He grabbed the train and got away. That was the last I saw or heard of him for quite a while.

"But he always left a trail of blood and bones behind him,

31

so after a while I managed to pick up his trail again. Followed him to Boquillas, Mexico. He had a hangout south of the Border and was working both sides of the river. Details don't matter, but again I managed to bust up his gang. Of course I was sort of fracturing international law by working south of the Rio Grande, but figured I could get by with it, under the circumstances."

Sheriff Carter's shrewd old eyes twinkled suddenly as Slade paused to roll and light a cigarette, but he said nothing and waited expectantly.

"I chased him north to the river," Slade resumed. "Again I thought I had him, but I didn't. From Boquillas, Mexico, to Boquillas, Texas, an overhead conveyor system cable stretches across the Rio Grande from the south shore to the north. The cable services ore buckets from the Boquillas silver mines to Texas, where the ore is run north for smelting. That night the cable serviced something else. The river was at flood—no horse could swim it—and it looked like Sosna was cornered. He left his horse and went up the south conveyor tower like a squirrel and started across the river via the cable, hand over hand. I followed. I was overtaking him when he swung around and began throwing lead at me. I answered and got him in the arm. Down he went to the water, which swept him into Boquillas Canyon. Everybody said nobody could live through that canyon with the river in flood, but Sosna did."

"And then?" prompted the sheriff.

"And then," Slade continued, "he dropped plumb out of sight for a long time. But he didn't stay out of sight. I learned that he was operating in Texas, just east of the Big Bend country. He was preying on emigrant wagons from east Texas and Louisiana. Once again we had it out. And once again I succeeded in putting his bunch out of operation. Sosna I chased into the hills. I saw him try to jump his horse across a narrow gorge at least fifty feet deep with sheer sides. Horse didn't make it and down they went to the rocks. In the clear moonlight I saw him and the horse lying motionless on the rocks. I was certain he was dead, so certain that, not being in very good shape myself, I didn't try to find a way into the gorge and make sure. Guess the shock broke the horse's neck, but evidently Sosna was only stunned. At least he sure wasn't dead."

Slade stopped talking again to roll another cigarette. "Hope I'm not boring you with this rambling yarn," he said.

"I find it darned interesting, go on," replied the sheriff.

"Well, as I said, I was sure for certain he was dead. And I was plumb flabbergasted when I got word that he wasn't dead and was at work again over around El Paso. So I lit out after him again. Same old story, managed to smash his organization, but I didn't smash Sosna. I met him and his last horned toad in the mouth of a cave they were using for a hangout. I gave him a chance to surrender."

Once again Sheriff Carter's eyes twinkled.

"Didn't take it, eh?" he observed.

"He sure didn't," Slade said. "He went for his iron. I got his follower dead center, but Sosna had ducked behind him in the split second he had to act. He grabbed the corpse and held it in front of him as a shield. The light was to his back, I was facing it. I tried to get him over the dead man's shoulder. Instead, he got me, in the leg. Knocked me heels over tincup. As I went down, Sosna whipped around and ran out of the cave. I shot as I fell but was never sure if I nicked him, even though he did seem to stagger a mite. Anyhow he got his horse and by the time I managed to crawl out the cave he was just rounding a bend a quarter of a mile distant and, it seemed to me, headed for Mexico. I figured he was headed for the mountains of Sinaloa, perhaps, and planned to follow him."

"Did he?" asked the sheriff.

"He did not," Slade replied. "Instead he got a bunch together and started east across Mexico, raiding as he went. Nobody seemed able to stop him. When I got a line on him and what he was doing, I decided I might as well fracture international law again."

For the third time, Sheriff Carter's old eyes twinkled and he seemed to have difficulty biting back a grin. Slade was too absorbed in the recital of his misadventures to notice.

"So here we went again," Slade concluded. "Same monotonous course of events. Just missed hogtying him a few times. Followed him to Brownsville, Texas, and Matamoros across the Rio Grande in Mexico. There he'd gotten going strong. Was setting up as a liberator and organizing an army of *peons*. Looked for a while that he might foment a real uprising that would have meant trouble a-plenty for the Border country. I managed to stop that. Then, with the sheriff of the county, I again met Sosna face to face, almost, with the two followers he had with him. The two followers died. Sosna made it to his horse, with me after him. There was a small steamer just pulling away from the Matamoros wharf, headed for the Gulf. Sosna jumped his horse across twenty feet of water, landed on the deck, whipped from the saddle, fired a couple of shots and took over. I didn't get a chance to line sights with him. Down the river he went and that was the last I heard of him till I got word he had moved back here to his original stamping grounds. Naturally I ambled up here, too. Now we'll see. Maybe his luck will run out, if luck is the right word. I'm hoping he'll turn out to be human after all and make a slip."

For the fourth time the sheriff's eyes twinkled, and *El Halcón* got a jolt.

"Quite a yarn," Carter remarked. "And do you think he knows you're a Ranger?"

Slade stared. "Now how the devil did *you* catch on?" he demanded.

"Son," answered the sheriff, "I'm an old man, and I've been in the peace officer business, one way or another, for nigh onto thirty years. I've learned to notice things a bit, too. In the first place, an owlhoot doesn't give another owlhoot a chance to surrender when they meet face to face. In the second place, an owlhoot chasing another owlhoot in the course of a feudin' don't bother his head about bustin' international law, or any other law. Figured first off that the outlaw brand didn't fit you. Knew you couldn't be a sheriff or deputy or marshal and go sashayin' all over Texas; only a Ranger could have the authority to do that. Simple, eh?"

"Oh, sure, once you've showed it to me," Slade conceded dryly. "Yes, I'm one of McNelty's men."

From a cunningly concealed secret pocket in his broad leather belt he drew a gleaming silver star set on a silver circle, the feared and honored badge of the Texas Rangers, and passed it to the sheriff. Carter gazed at it a moment, nodded and returned it to its owner.

"Knew old Jim McNelty pretty well years back," he remarked. "Haven't seen him for quite a spell, though. Fine old jigger."

34

"He certainly is," Slade agreed as he restored the badge to its hiding place.

"And now?" Carter asked.

"Now," Slade replied, "my chore is to try and drop a loop on Veck Sosna, if he doesn't drop one on me first."

"Any notion where to look for him?"

"Not the slightest, at the moment," Slade said. "No telling where he might be—someplace least expected, the chances are. Wouldn't surprise me if he walked into the office."

"He'd better not if he knows what's good for him," Carter growled. "I won't give him any chance to surrender, on that you can bet your last peso. You'd better not next time, either."

Slade smiled and did not comment.

"Suppose we drop in at the Trail End for something to eat?" he suggested.

"My sentiments," agreed the sheriff. "All this palavering makes me hungry."

At the Trail End, which was already pretty well crowded, they found a convenient table where they could talk and gave their orders.

"Answering your question of a little while ago," Slade remarked, "I'm not at all sure but that Sosna does know I'm a Ranger, or at least suspects it. Not that that would make any difference to Sosna. To him a Ranger is just another jigger who can be mowed down by hot lead. And his ego is such that he believes he's more than a match for any man on earth.

"And," he added with a wry smile," there are times when he comes close to proving it so. Has just about made me believe it a few times."

"My money's on *El Halcón*," Carter declared cheerfully. "May take a while and a bit of conniving, but you'll get him, sooner or later. No doubt in my mind as to that."

"Thanks for your confidence, I hope it isn't misplaced," Slade replied, with a smile.

"It ain't," the old peace officer said with finality. "I only hope I'll have the luck to be in at the finish. Well, here comes our chuck, so we'll forget about Sosna and other owlhoots for a while."

A period of busy silence followed. Finally the sheriff pushed back his plate and hauled out his old black pipe. Slade rolled a cigarette.

When his pipe was going good, Carter glanced around and shook his grizzled head.

"Filling up already, and it's early," he remarked. "This is liable to be quite a night. Payday for the spreads and all the young hellions will be ambling to town. I aim to swear in half a dozen specials for duty tonight. You're still sworn in, if it should happen to come in handy for some reason or other. Places like this ain't likely to be too bad, but those rumholes down toward the railroad and the lake! Gentlemen, hush!"

"Yes, it should be interesting down there," Slade agreed thoughtfully.

"Too darn interesting at times," grunted the sheriff. "Most anything can happen down there, and usually does."

After a bit, Carter knocked out his pipe. "Guess I'd better be getting back to the office," he announced. "Got to round up my specials. Be seeing you later."

SIX

THE AFTERNOON wore on, an unrolling scroll of light and fragrance. Flecks of shadow curdled in the cup of the amarillo flowers blanketing the prairie, from which the lake took its name. Behind the distant New Mexico mountains the sun sank in flaming glory. The blue veil of the dusk shrouded the rangeland. Blank windows alchemized to squares and rectangles of ruddy gold. Overhead, the silver roses of the sky bloomed in splendor, and it was night.

But there was no hush of peaceful dark in Amarillo. What was later to be known as the Queen City of the Panhandle proceeded to live up to its present designation, the Cowboy Capital of the Plains.

Every hitchrack was lined with horses. The board sidewalks were crowded. All the saloons were already doing plenty of business. Amarillo was beginning to rumble. Later the rumble would become a roar. Still later, a screeching howl. The payday bust! Sweat and toil and blood forgotten. Now it was whisky, cards, and girls. Young men lusty with life, carefree, reckless. And Walt Slade knew that at heart he was one of their number. The hard facts of life and the stern hand of duty curbed him somewhat, but not altogether. His pulses were quickening, the devils of laughter in the depths of his cold eyes edging their way to the front. He had a chore to do, and he'd spend most of the night seeking a way to do it; but just the same he was affected by the spirit of celebration that was abroad and resolved to try and snatch a mite of relaxation and enjoyment if possible.

The Trail End was rowdy and boisterous but, Slade decided, fairly innocuous, at least in the earlier hours of the night. Later, when the red-eye began to get in its licks it might be different. Most of the patrons, at present, were fresh-faced young cowhands from the neighboring spreads, ready for a fight, a frolic, or a footrace, but with no real harm in them.

Four husky floor men circulated among the crowd with watchful eyes for potential trouble, which they could usually stop before it really got started. And Swivel himself, Slade felt, was a salty hombre, and he quickly concluded that his nickname was not a misnomer; his eyes did swivel in all directions, continually, and he was the first to spot a possible row and first to forestall it.

So Slade found himself a small vacant table in a corner near the dance floor, ordered a drink, rolled a cigarette and eased back comfortably in his chair to survey the colorful scene.

It was colorful, all right, a typical payday night in a Border cowtown. With a charm all its own. The charm of gay recklessness that counted not the cost. Life, which might well be short, lived to the full for a few fleeting hours. Tomorrow? Why bother about that? Let the bubble of pleasure burst in the hand. It was lovely while it lasted. Sufficient unto eternity was the glory of the hour.

But while absorbed in his kaleidescopic surroundings, he nevertheless kept a watch on the swinging doors of the saloon, and not a man entered he did not note and try to evaluate. He hardly thought that Sosna or some of his followers would put in an appearance at the Trail End, but he was taking no chances. Would be like the unpredictable devil to do just that.

His effrontery was colossal and at times he achieved his ends by sheer audacity.

A lanky, leathery-faced individual strolled in, paused and glanced keenly around the room. Slade recognized Bill Harley, the sardonic-looking deputy sheriff. Harley's gaze centered on him and he sauntered over to the table.

"Take a load off your feet and have a drink," Slade invited, beckoning a waiter. Harley nodded acceptance and drew up a chair. He glanced around complacently.

"Place is really hopping," he remarked. "Same down by the lake and the railroad. Be trouble down there before the night is over is my bet. A gathering of prime specimens down there, not all of 'em cowhands even though they look to be. Especially in a rumhole called the Washout. The sort on the lookout for pickin's. Carter has a couple of specials circulating there but they got a lot of territory to cover, and those hellions usually manage to pull something where they ain't."

"The Washout?" Slade repeated interrogatively. Harley nodded again.

"Uh-huh," he replied, sampling his drink. "Real close to where the lake reaches when she's high. Be a good notion if it did get washed out. Places like this one are okay, plenty of heck raising and a rukus now and then but no undercover stuff likely to be pulled here. But places like the Washout! We could sure do without them."

He tossed off his glass, beckoned the waiter and ordered another round, which they consumed slowly. Suddenly he chuckled.

"There goes Swivel-eye into the back room with another poke of dinero," he remarked. "He took back a couple while I was here before. That old strongbox of his must be stuffed. It's a big night."

Shoving his empty glass aside, he beckoned the waiter, paid for the round and stood up.

"Guess I'd better be moseying around," he said. "Carter wants us on our toes tonight. He seems to think something really bad might happen."

"He could be right," Slade agreed.

"Yep, could be," said Harley. "Be seeing you." He sauntered out, his keen eyes shooting glances in every direction.

A hard man and one who didn't miss any bets, was Slade's conclusion.

El Halcón was growing restless and he decided he'd emulate Harley's example and stroll around a bit. The Washout! Somehow, the name was intriguing. Doubtless because of what Harley had said about the place. He paid his score and left the saloon, noting absently that Swivel-eye was nowhere in sight and that the door to the back room was closed. Doubtless he was counting the take, and from the way gold pieces were ringing on the mahogany, it was likely something of a chore.

The Trail End was two doors from the corner of a rather dimly lighted side street. Slade walked to the corner and turned into the side street. A few steps brought him to the mouth of a dark alley. He glanced up it, noted a pencil of light that evidently came from the crack of a partially closed door. And he judged from its distance from the alley mouth that the door was the back door of the Trail End, which opened onto the alley. He was slightly surprised that the owner should have left it open while stowing the money in the safe. And as he gazed at the bright streamer an instant he heard a sound that he quickly catalogued as the impatient stamp of a horse somewhere up the dark alley.

Funny place for a horse to be left, with plenty of hitching space available out front. Slade experienced a sudden stirring of curiosity. He hesitated an instant, then strolled up the alley.

As he surmised, the slightly open door was really that of the Trail End. He paused beside it, peered through the narrow opening, and stiffened to alert attention. He had a view of about half the room and when he saw tensed every nerve for instant action.

Swivel-eye Sanders lay on the floor, his face streaked with blood. In the far corner was a big iron safe, the door open. Two men squatted beside the safe, busily transferring its contents to a couple of canvas sacks.

Drawing both guns, Slade hit the door with his shoulder and leaped into the room. His voice blared at the pair—"Elevate!"

The two men came to their feet like cats, hurtling sideways, going for their guns, ducking and dodging.

Slade shot with both hands, left and right. Answering lances

39

of flame gushed toward him. A bullet whispered in his ear.

Another ripped the brim of his hat. Ducking and dodging himself, he fired again and again.

He sensed rather than saw a flicker of shadow on his left, going backward in a panther bound, he snapped a shot at a man looming in the doorway. There was a yelp of pain, the clatter of a falling gun, and the intruder vanished. Slade whirled to face the others, gun muzzles jutting forward.

Abruptly he realized there was nothing more to shoot at. Two motionless forms lay on the floor beside Swivel-eye, who was rolling his bloody head from side to side and muttering with returning consciousness. Slade raced to the door, peered cautiously, then stepped out. As he did so, he heard a clatter of fast hoofs in the darkness of the alley. He fired twice at the sound, paused to listen. The beat of hoofs was dimming into the distance. He returned to the room, where he found Swivel-eye sitting up, looking dazed.

"W-where the devil did you come from?" he mouthed. His eyes flashed with apprehension.

"Those two devils—" he began.

"They're taken care of," Slade interrupted. "How you feel?"

"Not too bad," Swivel-eye replied.

The tumult in the saloon had abruptly stilled. Now it burst forth anew. Somebody was hammering on the locked door.

"Hold it a minute till I open the door before somebody breaks it down," Slade said. He crossed to the door, unlocked it and swung it open to come face to face with Swivel-eyes head bartender who began yammering questions.

"Come in here," Slade told him. "The rest of you stay out till I tell you to come in," he told the crowd and closed and locked the door.

The barkeep was staring in amazement, his mouth hanging open. Swivel-eye, who apparently was again in command of his faculties, glared at him.

"Who the blankety-blank-blank left that back door unlocked?" he bawled.

"It—it was locked when I came on this afternoon, I tried it," stammered the barkeep. "There's the key hanging on the nail."

"Well, it wasn't locked when those two hellions barged in and belted me with a gun barrel," roared Swivel-eye. "Just

40

wait till I find out who left it unlocked! I'll pistol whip him within an inch of his life and then fire him."

"Don't go off half-cocked," Slade cautioned. "Perhaps somebody got hold of a duplicate key. That's an old-fashioned lock and not hard to open by somebody who knows how."

Again there was a pounding on the door. "Open it," Slade ordered.

The bartender did so and Sheriff Carter strode in.

"What the jumpin' blue blazes?" he demanded.

"Thieves! that's what!" shouted Swivel, one eye glaring, the other leering waggishly. "Where the blankety-blank were you fellers who're supposed to keep such things from happening? If it wasn't for Slade here they'd have got away with it. Why—"

Slade took charge again. "Simmer down," he advised, stemming Swivel-eye's tirade. "Think you can stand up?"

"Lend me a hand," growled Swivel-eye. With Slade's help he got to his feet, to stand weaving a little. Slade led him to a chair which hadn't been knocked to pieces and made him sit down.

"I want to give your head a once-over," he said. "Not much of a cut, but it bled freely."

With sensitive fingertips he explored the vicinity of the wound.

"No signs of fracture, so far as I can see," he announced. "Lucky you've got such thick hair; otherwise you might have been hurt a lot worse. Is there bandage and salve anywhere around?"

"I've got some in a drawer back of the bar," said the drink juggler.

"Get them," Slade said. "Keep the crowd out, Brian," he told Sheriff Carter.

Very quickly the barkeep returned with the medicants. Slade deftly padded and bandaged the wound. He rolled and lit a cigarette and handed it to Sanders, who gratefully took a couple of deep drags.

"That'll hold you till Doc Beard gets here," Slade said. "Send for him, Brian. Best not to take chances with a head wound. I'm not a doctor and may have missed something."

"I doubt it," growled Swivel-eye. "I don't think you ever miss anything."

41

Sheriff Carter opened the door and called a name. A swamper got his powders and hurried out to fetch the doctor.

"And now," Slade suggested to Sanders, "suppose you tell us just what happened."

"I'd just finished counting the take and was stashing it in the safe when I heard something behind me," Swivel-eye replied. "I turned around and saw those two devils swooping down on me. Next I saw was stars and comets and the roof falling in on me. If I can just find out who left that back door unlocked!" Slade crossed to the door in question and closed and locked it, using the key which hung on a nearby nail. Withdrawing the key from the lock, he looked it over carefully before replacing it on the nail.

"Not hard to duplicate by somebody who knows locks," he commented. "Of course somebody *may* have carelessly forgotten to lock the door. Brian, let's give those two carcasses a once-over. There was a third hellion in on it; I figure he was holding the horses up the alley. He very nearly did for me, but I managed to nick him in the arm, I think. Anyhow, he dropped his gun and skalleyhooted. There's the gun lying beside the door. I don't think I shot it out of his hand."

He picked up the gun and examined it. "Nope, slug didn't touch it," he said. "Must have gotten him in the arm. Not enough to stop him, though; he sure sifted sand. Now for the bodies."

The dead robbers were hard looking specimens, swarthy of complexion, with black eyes. Both were stocky but powerfully built.

"Comancheros, I'd be willing to wager," Slade muttered to Carter, who was turning out the pockets to reveal nothing of significance other than a considerable sum of money.

"Sosna's bunch?" the sheriff muttered back.

"Very likely," Slade replied. "Tell you more later."

The doctor arrived, white-bearded, frosty-eyed. Without wasting words, he removed Slade's bandage and carefully examined the wound.

"Nothing to it," was his verdict. "Couldn't dent his skull with a cannon ball. Didn't even need to change the bandage, but I gotta do something to earn my pay. You did a good job of tying up, young feller," he added to Slade, one eyelid closing the merest trifle. "Surgeon's hands! All right, Sanders, go get drunk and try not to rob too many folks tonight, or pizen 'em with your cactus juice." With another half-wink at Slade he stalked out.

"Finest old feller that ever spit on the soil," said Swivel-eye, drawing on the second cigarette Slade rolled for him. "Him and Slade have a heap in common."

Slade smiled. "Let's go get a drink," he suggested to the sheriff.

"And everything on the house," said Swivel-eye. "Hope you drink her dry."

SEVEN

AT A TABLE where they could talk without interruption, the sheriff said, "And you really think those hellions belonged to Sosna's bunch?"

"Yes," Slade replied. "And I understand now why Sosna was here the other day. He was looking the place over and concluded the payday take would be worth making a try for. So he managed to get a wax impression of the back door keyhole, I'd say, and made a duplicate. No trick for him; he's a whizzer where locks are concerned. I doubt if there is a safe or vault in the section he couldn't open. Had his devils stationed in the alley tonight. They unlocked the door, opened it the merest crack and watched Sanders come in and open the safe to pack away the money he had taken from the tills. Saw the safe was loaded, slipped in and clubbed him over the head."

"And as Sanders said, if it hadn't been for you they would have gotten away with it," observed Carter. "How'd you figure out what was going on?"

"Mostly luck," Slade replied. "I saw the light seeping through the crack in the door and thought it was funny Sanders would have left that door open while he was stowing the money in the safe. Then I heard a horse stamp up the alley and thought that was a mite strange. Figured it wouldn't

43

hurt to investigate. Sort of in the nature of a hunch, and it paid off."

"It sure did," grunted the sheriff. "There was plenty in that box. A pity one of the pair you did for wasn't Sosna himself. Think he's in town tonight?"

"Not beyond the realm of possibility," Slade answered. "He may have something else lined up. Otherwise he probably would have been in on this chore. Although he does sometimes leave such routine business to subordinates he can depend on."

"Bet he'll be in a temper for fair when he hears about what happened," chuckled Carter.

"Quite likely," Slade replied, with a smile.

"Quite likely, too, that he's found out *El Halcón* is on his trail again, eh?"

"It is plausible to think so," Slade conceded.

"And will be out to even the score."

"Doubtless."

"You don't seem much bothered about it," growled the sheriff.

Slade shrugged his broad shoulders.

"Sosna and I must play the hand out."

Sheriff Carter sighed and shook his head. "Well, reckon I'd better go and arrange to have those carcasses packed to the office," he said. "More fodder for our local Boot Hill. Business is picking up since you landed in the section. Say! you've sure got everybody looking toward you, including all of the dance floor girls."

Slade laughed. "They won't look long," he predicted. "A few more drinks and they will have forgotten all about what happened. Just added a little spice of variety to the night's doings." The sheriff chuckled and sipped his drink.

El Halcón was right. Very quickly everything swung back to normal and the payday hilarity was going full blast. The only reminder of what had happened was the bandaged and thoroughly bad tempered Swivel-eye, who glowered at all and sundry with one orb and regarded jocosely with the other.

Meanwhile, Slade was doing some hard thinking. He wondered if Sosna had really been in town with his followers to whom he had relegated the chore of cleaning out the Trail End safe, and if he had some other nefarious operation in mind. Would be just like him. With the Trail End the focus

44

of interest, he might reason that there would be negligence somewhere else which would provide him with opportunity. Sosna was mighty good at sizing up opportunity and taking advantage of it.

The big question was where would he be most likely to strike, if he did strike. Slade wracked his brains for a possible answer to that question.

The bank? Hardly. Sheriff Carter had assigned two alert specials to keep an eye on that institution. So what else?

The question was still unanswered when Carter glanced at the clock over the bar and announced,

"Guess I'd better mosey over to the office and see if any reports have come in. Coming along?"

Slade shook his head. "I think I'll stick around for a while longer," he said. "May drop in at the office later, if you're still there."

"I'll be there for a while," Carter said. "Be seeing you." With a wave of his hand to Swivel-eye, he walked out.

Although he did not tell the sheriff so, Slade had already made up his mind to leave the Trail End for a while. He wanted to have a look at the lower town, around the lake and the railroad and did not inform Carter of his intentions because he knew he'd want to accompany him, and he preferred to make his tour of inspection alone.

Carter was almost sure to be recognized in any of the places down there and gentlemen of uneasy conscience would guard their speech. Going it alone, Slade hoped to possibly hear something said that would prove of value; alcohol opens lips that would otherwise be tightly latigoed. He also waved to Swivel-eye and sauntered out, glances following his progress. Walking a little ways down the street he paused and glanced back. Nobody had left the saloon. A few more steps and another backward glance. Satisfied that he was not wearing a tail, he turned toward the lower town.

Gradually the streets grew darker. There were fewer lighted windows and through the panes that were lighted the seepage of glow had a gray look, hinting at unwashed glass and smoky lamp chimneys. Here as elsewhere, the pay-day bust was going strong, the spirit of hilarity still manifest. But it seemed to Slade it had acquired a shriller note, like to the whine of an irritated owl, or even the sinister buzz of an aroused rattlesnake.

Slade walked warily, for here were the hangouts of the more sinister elements, the vultures who preyed on whatever victims chance might send their way. The vicious, the depraved, the furtive, the stealthily cunning. Here a drunken cowhand might well be found knocked on the head and his pockets turned inside out. Here a stacked deck in a card game was not uncommon. The dance floor girls were questionable, to put it mildly. The bartenders were not above slipping a soporific drop or two into the glass of a likely-looking prospect. And the victim, awakening unexpectedly, would be silenced by a knife thrust.

Altogether a veritable devil's brew. But one which, for various reasons, the visiting cowhands found attractive. That way in all such Border towns, Slade knew. And Amarillo was a Border town in the sense that it was one of the outposts of civilization in a wild land. So *El Halcón* walked warily, his keen eyes probing the shadows, his hands never very far from the butts of his guns.

Now he was nearing the point where the railroad curved around the lake, the final outskirts of the lower town. In view was the sparkle of the water, and the gleam of the twin steel ribbons stretching east and west.

Abruptly he slowed his pace, came to a halt. Across the street was a wide window that glowed a bit brighter than most. On the glass was legended in staring red letters—

THE WASHOUT

The place Deputy Bill Harley had mentioned in unfavorable terms. Over the swinging doors came strains of music, not too bad, the thump of boots and the click of high heels on the dance floor. The rumble of voices was punctuated by the clink of bottle necks on glasses and the sprightly ring of gold pieces on the "mahogany." Evidently the Washout was doing a good business.

After gazing a moment, Slade sauntered across the street and pushed his way through the swinging doors, casting an all embracing glance over the crowded room. Finding a place at the long bar, he ordered a drink and continued to survey the room by the back bar mirror. The Washout boasted a rather motley gathering, including many cowhands, railroaders, teamsters and some "store clothes" gents. All in all, not much different from the patrons of the better lighted and possibly more orderly places farther uptown. Slade felt that

46

Harley's estimate had been slightly colored by prejudice against the place, although he was ready to concede there was plenty of potential dynamite present.

The bartender who served him favored him with a keen and appraising scrutiny but was a affable enough. His entrance had attracted no more than the passing attention doubtless accorded any newcomer, so far as he was able to judge.

One group intrigued Slade's interest. Six men sat at a table near the door, drinking and playing a desultory game of cards. The majority, he noted, were inclined to swarthiness. Nothing particularly unusual about that in this section, though, where an infiltration of Indian blood was not uncommon. Also, there were quite a few Mexican sheep raisers in the Canadian Valley.

"I'm seeing Comancheros wherever there's a good case of sun-tan," he chuckled to himself.

It appeared that the group was expecting somebody or had some sort of an assignation in mind, for they kept glancing at the clock over the bar. However, they showed no signs of tension or repressed excitement; their glances were casual. He dismissed them for the moment and studied other occupants of the room. Gradually he became convinced that there was nothing out of the ordinary in the place, nothing that invited his serious attention. He finished his drink and strolled out. He hesitated a moment, then walked slowly to the railroad; the station was just a short distance to the east. To the west the tracks ran straight for better than a mile. As he gazed absently along their dwindling gleam, he heard the wail of a whistle thin with distance. Doubtless the night passenger train, the Tucumcari Flyer, which would pause briefly at Amarillo. He decided to watch her pull in, leaned against a convenient telegraph pole and rolled a cigarette.

Far to the west appeared a sparkle that swiftly grew larger, the locomotive headlight. Slade watched it increase in brilliance. Now he could hear the engine's exhaust, a loudening hum. The rails at his feet began to click. The train was not much more than half a mile distant, and already slowing for the station.

Suddenly the beam of the headlight was drowned by a blaze of yellowish flame. A moment later to Slade's ears came a muffled boom followed by a crashing sound. And at the

47

same instant, from the direction of the saloon he had just quitted erupted a bellow of gunfire and a wild shouting. Instinctively, he turned in that direction, then his gaze swung back to the west as there was another burst of flame followed by a louder boom.

The shooting and yelling in front of the saloon continued. The Washout, which had hushed for a couple of seconds, was now in an uproar; and echoing the banging of the guns, there drifted from the dark prairie to the west a sharp crackling as of thorns burning briskly under a pot.

More shooting, more yelling, then a clatter of fast hoofs fading eastward.

Men were boiling from the Washout and other places along the street, shouting, cursing, questioning. The whole end of town appeared aroused by the hullabaloo, attention focused on the vicinity of the Washout. And belatedly, Slade understood. He gazed westward an instant, where he could discern a dim gleam of lights, stationary. The locomotive headlight beam had vanished. Then he whirled, skirted the Washout, threaded his way swiftly through the groups of excited men and equally excited dance floor girls and raced uptown to the sheriff's office.

EIGHT

SHERIFF CARTER was standing in the door. He recognized *El Halcón* and shouted, "What the devil's going on down by the railroad, do you know? Sounded like a corpse-and-cartridge session for fair. I sent Harley and Wayne down there on the run."

"They won't find anything," Slade replied tersely. "Get your horse as fast as you can; we're riding west. And send somebody to the railroad telegraph office to tell the operator to summon the wreck train; it's needed. Send for Doc Beard;

48

the chances are he'll be needed, too. And leave word to your deputies to follow us."

"What in blazes are you talking about?" demanded the bewildered sheriff.

"That Sosna put one over on us, and a good one," Slade replied bitterly. "He just wrecked the Tucumcari Flyer a half mile or so out of town. Blew up the track with dynamite, in front of the locomotive. He did it once before up here, when he was operating in this section a few years back. Get your horse and I'll tell you the rest. I'm going after mine."

Spouting profanity, the sheriff headed for his own mount. Working at top speed, Slade got the rig on Shadow and rode back to the office.

"I see it all now, marvel of perspicacity," he remarked to Shadow, with sarcasm directed at himself. "Those horned toads in the Washout were keeping tabs on the clock for a good reason. They knew when the Flyer was due to arrive and slid out of there shortly after I did, not doubt. They waited around in front of the saloon till they heard the first dynamite blast, then cut loose with their phony gun battle to distract attention from what was happening out on the prairie. It worked, all right."

A few minutes later the sheriff arrived, mounted. "Everything taken care of," he said. "The nerve of that sidewinder, wrecking the train within sight of town!"

"Shrewd and farsighted," Slade replied. "He waited until he was slowing for the station and then set off his charge of dynamite under the rails. If he'd wrecked her when she was going full speed, there would have been the chance that the express car, which he was after, might have been a tangled mess of splintered wood and steel and the safe, perhaps, buried or in such a position it would have been impossible for him to get at it. As it was, the chances are only the engine left the rails."

"And that blasted gun fight was staged, of course?"

"Of course, to hold everybody's attention. It takes time, even for an expert cracksman like Sosna to open an express car safe. Had he not staged the fight as he did, attention would have been attracted to the wreck and with saddled and bridled horses standing at the hitchracks, he might well have had a bunch bearing down on him before he finished the chore. Oh, he has brains, and knows how to use them.

49

As it is, he will have accomplished what he set out to do and be gone before we get there."

They were riding steadily at a fast pace while they talked. Now the lighted coaches could be seen and soon they heard the hiss and rumble of escaping steam. Shortly afterward they dismounted beside the wreck.

As Slade predicted, the locomotive lay slantwise on its side in the hole the exploding dynamite had hollowed out. Splintered ties and twisted rails lay about. The express car had stayed on the iron, but its door was blown to bits, its windows shattered. Shattered, too, by the force of the explosion or gunfire were most of the coach windows. The passengers huddled together in talkative groups.

A blue-clad trainman hurried to meet them.

"Anybody badly hurt?" Slade asked.

"Not too bad," the railroader replied. "Just a God's mercy, though, that somebody wasn't killed. Those hellions let off bullets in every direction. The express messenger was knocked out when the dynamite they threw at it blew the door open, but he's got his senses back and seems okay. Engineer has a cut head, the fireman a scalded arm and some face cuts. A few cuts and bruises among the passengers."

"The doctor will be here shortly," Slade said. "Meanwhile I'll take a look at the engineer and fireman and see what can be done for them. You can tell the sheriff exactly what happened."

Without delay, he got to work on the engineer and fireman, deciding their hurts were not serious. A little ointment, a pad or two and some bandage from his saddle pouch took care of them. Before he had finished the chore, Doc Beard arrived, rumbling profanity, and took over. Slade drew the conductor aside.

"Did you notice how many were in the bunch?" he asked.

"Six or seven, I'd say," the con replied.

"Get a look at them?"

The con shook his head. "Not much of a one, only a peek," he said. "I stuck my head out the door and a slug fanned it; I ducked back and stayed back till they rode away. They were masked. One was mighty big and tall, sorta loomed over the others and seemed to be giving the orders. Every now and then one of 'em would send a bullet through a coach window

—sorta hinting it would be a good idea to stay inside and not look out. Folks got the general notion, all right."

"So I imagine," Slade smiled. "Come on, Brian," he said to the sheriff. "Let's have a look inside the express car."

The inside of the express car was something of a mess; the floor was covered with broken glass and splintered wood. The door of the safe stood open. The combination knob lay on the floor beside it.

The messenger was sitting in a chair, still looking a mite dazed.

"How you feel?" Slade asked.

"Not too bad except I'm a bit woozy," the messenger replied.

"Did you see anything of what went on in here?"

The messenger shook his head vigorously. "Seemed the sky fell in on me when that dynamite cut loose against the door. The next thing I knew, Earl, the conductor, was shaking me. Reckon I was out for quite a while."

"You're lucky not to be out for good," Slade said grimly. "Sosna must be getting a mite soft," he observed to the sheriff. "Didn't kill anybody, which is unusual for him. Guess he didn't want to waste the time."

The sheriff swore. The messenger shivered. Slade gestured to the combination knob lying beside the safe.

"Drilled it out, the Sosna touch," he said. "Didn't risk knocking it off with a sledge, which would have been faster but with a chance of jamming the tumblers. And look at those drill holes, set with micrometer precision. Yes, it was Sosna, all right, no doubt as to that."

He turned back to the messenger. "Know how much they got?" he asked.

"Better'n thirty thousand," the messenger replied. "Old box was loaded today."

"You don't usually pack that much?"

"Very seldom," the messenger said. "This was a sorta unusual day. Nobody was supposed to know about it, of course."

Slade nodded but did not comment. Veck Sosna always seemed able to learn what he was not supposed to learn. Could have been just coincidence, but Slade didn't think so; Sosna's gambles were usually on a sure thing. He always knew in advance just what he was going after.

In fact, the real objective for the attempted robbery of

51

the Trail End saloon was now quite obvious, Slade felt. That, too, was to create a diversion, to concentrate attention on the saloons. Of course Sosna would know that the Trail End would very likely provide a nice haul, but nothing compared to what he tied onto by the train robbery. Well, he had outsmarted himself a little, at the cost of two men. Not that it would bother him much; he could get plenty more followers. But being outsmarted, as he undoubtedly would figure he was, would not suit the outlaw leader any too well. Especially coming on the heels, as it were, of his misadventure following the stage robbery. Very soon, Sosna would be in a very bad temper. Which, Slade hoped, might work to his advantage.

Just the same, he felt that he, too, had been outsmarted. If he'd just tumbled to why the hellions in the Washout were watching the clock he might have thwarted the train robbery. Sosna always seemed a jump ahead of him.

Which, strictly speaking, was not true. He, Slade, had anticipated and frustrated more than one of Sosna's operations. But the disquieting fact remained—Sosna was still on the loose, still defying capture.

Old Doc Beard came clambering into the car, looking more irascible than ordinary. "All right, Pete, I'll give you a once-over and see if your brains are addled," he said. "If they ain't, you're in an abnormal condition for you and will need treatment."

A brief examination appeared to satisfy him as to the messenger's condition.

"Still loco as a coot, so you have nothing to worry about," he said. "Fee? What fee? A fee for telling you what everybody knows, that you're half-witted? Go get drunk and forget it. Now I've got to go see if those scratched passengers are all set to bring suit against somebody."

He bounced out of the car with an agility that would have done credit to one forty years younger.

"He delivered me when I was born," Pete chuckled as he gratefully accepted a cigarette from Slade. "Told my mother Darwin was right, only the process sometimes worked backward. Finest old jigger that ever saved a life. Pretends to be hard and tough, but at heart he's soft as melted butter. The sort of results the Good Lord gets when He sets out to do a real bang-up chore."

Both Slade and the sheriff nodded emphatic agreement.

"Well, guess we've done all we can here," the Ranger observed to Carter. "So long, Pete, better follow the doctor's advice."

"I do feel the need of a snort right now," Pete admitted, with a grin.

"You don't feel the need of one any more than I do," growled the sheriff. "And when I hit town I'm going to get it. Blazes! what a night."

"Did your deputies make it okay?" Slade asked as they left the car.

"They're circulating among the passengers, asking questions, but the chances are they won't learn much," replied the sheriff. He glanced around, gestured toward a straggle of growth near the right-of-way.

"Reckon that's where the hellions holed up to wait for the train," he remarked.

"Wouldn't be surprised if they're there right now, laughing at us," Slade said cheerfully.

The sheriff jumped, and cast an apprehensive glance toward the thicket. Slade glanced around himself.

"See quite a few folks have ridden out from town for a look-see," he commented. "Really, though, they might be among them, would be just like the Sosna bunch."

"Oh, shut up!" snorted Carter. "You'll have me looking sideways at everybody. Let's go get that snort. Guess the wreck train will make it here before long."

"About an eighty-mile run, but they'll highball," Slade answered. "Here come the deputies. Learn anything, boys?"

"Judging from what those loco coots have to say, there were at least three hundred outlaws and a band of Comanches," Harley replied disgustedly.

"Hot lead through a window over your head tends to promote exaggeration," Slade smiled.

"I reckon, whatever that means," Harley sighed as he swung into the saddle. "First stop the Trail End and a snort of red-eye, right?"

"My sentiments," grunted the sheriff. "Let's go!"

Upon reaching the Trail End, they were bombarded with questions, which Harley and the sheriff answered profanely. After which they found a table and ordered their snort. Slade settled for coffee.

"And now I'm going to bed," he announced as he pushed

back his empty cup. "It's getting close to daylight and things are quieting down. I doubt if there'll be any more excitement tonight. Suppose Doc will hold an inquest tomorrow, right?"

"Oh, sure, some time in the afternoon," Carter replied. "Be seeing you."

Waving goodnight to Swivel-eye, Slade left the saloon and headed for the stable, which he reached without incident. After making sure that Shadow was properly cared for, and cleaning and oiling his guns, he tumbled into bed and slept soundly until noon, awakening refreshed and hungry.

NINE

BEFORE DESCENDING the stairs to bathe and shave, he rolled a cigarette and sat gazing across the sun drenched prairie and reviewing recent happenings.

In that flood of golden light, his accomplishments looked better than the night before. After all, he didn't do so bad. He frustrated one robbery and downed two of the three robbers. He could hardly be held to account for not anticipating the express car robbery. That would have meant the exercising of a gift of clairvoyance not accorded humanity in general.

"Although I have some Scotch blood, I guess I haven't enough to be endowed with the second sight," he told the glowing tip of his cigarette. "But I'm darned if I don't sometimes believe that Sosna has. The way he manages to learn things is positively uncanny. But then Veck Sosna is uncanny in more ways than one. Oh, well, his luck should run out some time—I hope."

In a cheerful frame of mind he went downstairs, cleaned up and after a word with Shadow sallied forth in search of some breakfast. Doc Beard would hardly hold the inquest before the middle of the afternoon and he had plenty of time.

So he proceeded to enjoy a leisurely meal spiced with cigarettes and thought.

While he was eating, Swivel-eye Sanders came in, still bandaged but otherwise looking not too bad for wear. He sauntered over to Slade's table and sat down.

"I won't forget what you did for me last night, feller," he said. "You saved me a hefty passel of dinero and the devil knows what else. If I'd happened to rouse up while those devils were still there they might have silenced me for good. I'd hand you a mite of a helpin' from the safe, but I know better than to offer it to you. One thing I insist on, though, if we're going to stay friends."

"What's that?" Slade asked, with a smile.

"That when you come in here, everything is on the house," Swivel replied with emphasis.

"Well, the way you put it, I guess I can hardly refuse to accept your hospitality," Slade chuckled. "I'll promise not to overdo it."

"Huh! from the way you drink, it's hardly worth putting on the tab," said Swivel-eye. He chuckled in turn.

"Too many gents I know would go right ahead and drink themselves into an early grave. Well, guess I'd better mosey around and see if everything is under control. Doc is going to hold his inquest at three and wants me to be there. Order anything you want, the more the better."

Thanking Swivel-eye again, Slade took advantage of the offer to the extent of a final cup of steaming coffee. After which, with time to kill, he wandered down to the lake front.

Pausing at the Washout, he found it appearing quite innocuous by daylight. On the lake shore he stood looking out over the placid sheet of water. The former site of the stockyards and other buildings was now quite dry, but as he gazed across the stretch of land, Slade shook his head. Henry Sanborn was apparently okay as a promoter, but as an engineer and geologist he lacked a good deal. How the devil, Slade wondered, examining the terrain with the eye of a geologist, did he fail to recognize the fact that all that stretch of land had been under water time and again.

Shortly before the death of his father, which occurred after financial reverses that entailed the loss of the elder Slade's ranch, young Walt had graduated from a famous college of engineering. He had planned to take a postgraduate course in special subjects to round out his education and better fit him for the profession of engineering, which he intended to make his life's work.

At the moment, however, the postgrad had been economically impossible. While he was pondering what his next move would be, he dropped in on Captain Jim McNelty, his father's friend. Captain Jim listened with interest as Slade explained his dilemma.

"Walt," the Ranger captain said, "I have a suggestion to make. Why don't you join the Rangers for a while and study in spare time, of which you'll have plenty for your purpose? You seemed to like the chore when you worked with me some during summer vacations. What say?"

Considering the proposition, pro and con, Slade concluded that the notion was a good one and signed up with Captain Jim. Long since he had gotten as much, and more, as he would have hoped for from the postgrad. Meanwhile, however, Ranger work had gotten a strong hold on him, presenting as it did endless opportunities for helping others and making the world a better place for decent people to live in. He hesitated to sever connections with the illustrious body of law enforcement officers. At least not just yet. He was young and there was plenty of time to be an engineer; he'd stick with the Rangers for a while yet.

So to Slade it was plain that the land on which he gazed had often been submerged and always would be in time of heavy rains. Oldtimers could have told Sanborn so. Why didn't they?

The answer to that, however, was not particularly hard to come by. The oldtimers resented Sanborn and his plans for a town and evidently figured that, given enough rope, he would eventually hang himself.

Which was all very well except for one drawback—Mr. Sanborn didn't hang easily. He got his town, and it was a going concern. Later, when he fenced his big ranch with barbed wire, the oldtimers were still more disgruntled, but unable to do anything about it.

Reflecting on the vagaries of the oldtimers, Slade strolled back uptown and was on time for the inquest.

The inquest was a formality, no more. Slade was commended for doing a good chore and regret was expressed that apparently one of the hellions got away. Better luck next

56

time. Doc Beard banged his gavel, the undertaker rubbed his hands together complacently, and Boot Hill got a couple more tenants.

A satisfactory conclusion to the incident. That is, for all except possibly the prime exhibits, whose reactions might well be dubious. Slade and the sheriff retired to his office to talk things over.

There was not a great deal to talk about. The conversation consisted chiefly in speculation as to where Sosna would be likely to strike next, and how, if possible, to thwart him.

"So far everybody has been lucky," Slade observed. "In his last two raids he didn't kill anybody, which is unusual for him. That won't last; there is a grave probability that next time somebody will die. Sosna is not in the habit of leaving witnesses."

Sheriff Carter swore wearily. "I'm scared you're right," he conceded. "What the devil are we going to do?"

"I think," Slade said slowly, "that my best bet is to go looking for Sosna instead of waiting until he shows up somehow. I'm positive that he has a hangout somewhere in the Canadian River Valley. If I can locate his hangout, I may get a chance to drop a loop on him."

"Or get one dropped on you," grunted the sheriff. "Like walking into a den of rattlesnakes."

"All you need to do is see the snake first and you're okay," Slade replied cheerfully.

"Uh-huh, but sometimes that takes considerable seeing. Don't you think you'd better take somebody with you? Bill Harley would be glad to go."

"One has a better chance to escape detection than two," Slade objected. "I think I'll do better going it alone."

"You may be right," the sheriff conceded, adding, "But just the same you'll be taking one devil of a chance. Going to leave right away?"

Slade shook his head. "No, I'll wait until well after dark, make it to the Valley before daybreak and hole up there until it gets light. I used to know a few folks down there and perhaps I can contact somebody from whom information might be obtained. Most of the Valley dwellers are too afraid of Sosna to do any talking, but now and then you run across somebody who isn't, and would like to see him get his comeuppance. The last time I was here, in the course of my

57

initial contact with Sosna, an old Mexican who lives in the Valley gave me the tip that enabled me to follow him to the Trail of Tears and the hidden valley in the Cap Rock hills. May get another break if I manage to contact the right person. Worth giving a try, anyhow."

"Sounds reasonable," Carter agreed. "Well, all I can say is good luck and good hunting."

"Thanks," Slade said. "I'll need all the good luck I can tie onto, no doubt about that."

"Aim to drop in at Tascosa?" the sheriff asked.

"I wouldn't be surprised," Slade answered. "Things are sort of on the downgrade there, a condition that often attracts the riff-raff. Could possibly learn something there."

"Could be," Carter conceded. "Tascosa has been sort of slipping since the railroad they expected bypassed her and it looks like the other line will, too. And with the big ranches to the south fencing her in and not allowing the trail herds from farther south to pass over their holdings, which they have to do to reach Tascosa. That's one of the reasons why Amarillo is booming. But Tascosa is still plenty wooly, although I reckon she won't last many more years. Yep, plenty wooly, with all sorts of salty characters showing up there and raising heck. Yep, you might be able to learn something in Tascosa, if you decide to go there."

"Chances are I will, later," Slade said. "First I want to have a look at the lower Valley. If I don't learn anything there I'll likely give Tascosa a whirl."

It was nearing midnight when Slade rode out of Amarillo. As was to be expected the night after the big payday bust, the streets were practically deserted, windows dark. A mile or so out of town he drew rein and for some time sat gazing back the way he had come. Confident he was not wearing a tail, he rode on, north by slightly west, the most direct route to the great Canadian River Valley, his objective.

In his saddle pouches was a store of staple provisions, along with a small skillet and a little flat bucket. As to whether he would camp out the first morning and catch forty winks under a tree depended on a contact he hoped to make.

"If the old jigger isn't dead, and I doubt he is, I figure we'll find him right where we left him a few years back," he told Shadow. "If we do, I'll sleep soft and you'll put away a hefty helpin' of oats."

The Canadian Valley was a rough, broken trough several hundred feet lower than the prairie lands north and south of it. In the center of the Valley is a temperamental river fed by springs and tributaries. During the dry season its bed is a floor of gleaming sand, along which winds a narrow ribbon of running water. In times of flood it is a surging, mad, debris-strewn torrent. Treacherous quicksands make fording a risky business.

At present the Canadian was low and Slade anticipated no difficulty in crossing it if he decided to do so.

It was still dark when he reached the lip of the Valley, although the east was flushing pink, but sure-footed Shadow negotiated the descent through the tangle of chaparral without much difficulty. Now he rode directly west, for he knew there was a trail, or what passed for one, running along the south bank of the river, and for that trail he was headed.

By the time he sighted it, birds were caroling in the thickets, the stars had turned from gold to silver and were winking out, the sky brightening. A little breeze shook down a myriad glowing dew gems. Slade turned Shadow's head due west and rode on through a world all glorious with morning.

Rounding a bend, he sighted a lonely adobe with a garden patch fronting it. Nearby grazed a few sheep and goats. Bending over the garden patch was a wizened figure.

"It's him, all right," Slade chuckled to Shadow. "He'll live to be a hundred!" He raised his voice in a shout—

"*Buenos dias, amigo!* Have you a bed for a sleepy hombre?"

The figure straightened, turned, to reveal an old Mexican who peered at the lone horseman with outthrust neck. He uttered a glad cry—

"*Capitan!* Is it really you, come back to me?"

"*Si*, Estaban, it's me, and I've returned," Slade replied as he rode closer, dismounted, and held out his hand, which the old man shook warmly.

"And the beautiful *caballo!*" Estaban chattered. "Ha! he remembers me!"

"Why shouldn't he?" Slade countered. "The last time he was here you stuffed him with oats till he was like to burst."

Estaban chuckled and stroked Shadow's glossy neck. "And stuff him again I will," he declared. "And you, *Capitan*, doubtless you hunger and thirst. First we will place the *caballo* in the stable with my mule Carmencita—you remember Carmencita, of course—and care for all his wants. Then we will prepared a feast fit for the occasion."

He led the way to a small stable back of the cabin, which was occupied by a friendly and pensive looking mule, chattering away in the precise English of the Mission-taught Mexican. After Shadow was cared for they entered the cabin, where Estaban at once got busy over the stove.

"First the coffee, steaming hot," he said, pouring Slade a cup. "Then a meal for the honored guest. For *El Halcón*, the kindly, the compassionate, the good, the friend of the lowly."

"Thank you, Estaban," Slade replied as he accepted the coffee.

The meal, when it was forthcoming, was all Estaban claimed for it, and to it the Ranger did full justice. It was some time before he pushed back his empty plate with a sigh of satisfaction and rolled a cigarette. The old Mexican shot him a keen glance.

"Capitan," he said, "your eyes are heavy; you must rest. Later we will talk."

He gestured to a small inner room. "Where you slept when last you were here," he remarked. "I will make ready the bed."

Feeling quite weary, Slade gratefully accepted and stretched out on the comfortable bunk. Very quickly he was sound asleep and did not awaken until early afternoon.

Slade did not get up immediately, but for a while lay thinking. He considered himself fortunate in finding Estaban alive and well. The old Mexican was shrewd; not much went on in the Valley which he didn't know about. If Sosna was in the Valley, it was quite likely Estaban had heard of his presence, might even know where he could be found. With this in mind he arose and joined the old man in the outer room. After a dip in the cold waters of the nearby river and a shave he was ready for the bountiful breakfast Estaban had prepared.

While he ate, the old man sat smoking a husk cigarette and regarding him in silence which he did not break until Slade had finished eating. Then—

"El Halcón has returned. And returned, too, his great enemy, the outlaw Sosna."

60

Slade rolled a cigarette and lit it. "Know anything, Estaban?" he asked.

Estaban puffed hard on his own *cigarillo* before replying. His eyes grew retrospective.

"While *Capitan* slept, I rode," he said. "Five miles to the west is a small plaza where live men who never seem to work but who always have money, much money, with which they gamble among themselves. One who is my *amigo* watched and saw. He thought it strange that men who do so little should have *dinero* in such quantity. What does *El Capitan* think?"

"I think, Estaban," Slade replied, "that you may have hit on something. Looks a bit that way to me. He didn't mention seeing Sosna?"

"He knows not the man Sosna, and him I did not discuss," Estaban answered. "I thought it wise not to do so."

"Chances are you were right," Slade conceded. "Five miles to the west, you say?"

"That is right. Near the river bank. Long ago one lived there who grew vegetables for sale. Now, however, his garden is overrun by the chaparral, from which my *amigo* watched the men gamble on a table in front of the cabin door."

"The vicinity of the cabin is heavily brush grown, eh?"

"It is so," Estaban replied.

"Nobody else lives in the plaza?"

"No one anymore; it has been deserted for years. Only recently, I heard, did those men come there to live."

"Begins to look like a likely set-up, and made to order," Slade observed musingly.

"You plan to ride there, *Capitan*?" Estaban asked.

"I think I will, after dark," Slade replied. "I'd like to have a look at those gents, without them getting a look at me. From the way you describe the place, it shouldn't be too much of a chore, and it might get results."

"You believe they are Sosna's men?"

"It's not beyond the realm of possibility," Slade said. "And if so, there's the chance that Sosna himself will show up there, sooner or later."

"Quite likely," Estaban agreed.

"Do those jiggers ever ride this way?" Slade asked.

"I have never seen them," the Mexican answered. "I would say it is doubtful. There are easier ways to leave the Valley farther west, beyond that plaza. And there the Tucumcari Trail is close."

"I see," Slade nodded. "And there wouldn't be much danger of meeting them on the way from here to the plaza. Yes, I think I'll take me a little ride tonight and try and investigate that plaza. Really it looks like a good lead. You've been a big help, Estaban."

The old man bowed his gray head. "It is an honor to be of service to *El Halcón*," he replied.

TEN

IT WAS WELL past dark when Slade said *hasta luego to* Estaban and rode west. He rode at a leisurely pace and very much on the alert, for there was always the chance that for some reason or other the dubious denizens of the plaza cabin might take a notion to ride east. And he preferred not to meet all six of them bulging around a bend.

Slade had ridden the trail before, as far west as Tascosa, and had a fair idea as to where the plaza in question was located. So after a while he slowed Shadow to a walk, his irons making but a whisper of sound on the soft surface of the trail, and his vigilance increased as he carefully estimated the distance he had covered since leaving Estaban's cabin. He knew he must be getting pretty close to his goal.

It was the pungent whiff of wood smoke that informed him that he was indeed very close, and abruptly, as he slowly rounded a bend, he saw a sparkle of light ahead.

Pulling Shadow to a halt, he sat for several moments gazing at the wan glow which apparently came from a window in need of washing. Another moment and he dismounted.

"Into the brush for you," he whispered to his mount. "Can't take a chance on your kicking a rock or a fallen branch."

Leading the horse through the screen of chaparral, which

wasn't very thick at the point, he dropped the split reins to the ground, gave him a pat and then drifted silently as a shadow through the growth until he was opposite the cabin. Worming his way forward he peered out cautiously. To his ears came a rumble of voices, and through the open door he could make out figures moving about.

He earnestly desired a look through the window, but with the door standing wide open it would be devilishly risky to attempt it.

While he was debating the matter with himself, the light suddenly went out. Instantly alert, he eased farther back into the growth and stood with his hands hovering over the butts of his guns, wondering what it might portend.

However, the unemotional sound of voices continued and a moment later six men filed from the cabin, closing the door behind them. They skirted the cabin and walked unhurriedly to the back, where they disappeared. Slade stood watchful, wondering what they had in mind. He felt positive that they had not sighted him and were circling about to take him from the rear, but it wasn't impossible that they had. The sort Veck Sosna gathered together never lacked for shrewdness and perhaps the sauntering and the casual conversation were in the nature of a blind.

He felt relieved when, a few minutes later, the sextet reappeared, mounted. Again they skirted the cabin, turned and rode west along the trail at a leisurely pace.

Without hesitation, Slade acted. He hurried back to Shadow, led him to the trail and mounted. Peering through the gloom, he sent the big black west in the wake of the six cabin occupants. With his unusually keen eyesight he believed he could keep them in view without being spotted himself. At any rate he'd try, for he was consumed with curiosity as to just what they were up to. There was a chance they were keeping a rendezvous with Sosna himself, who was certainly not one of their number.

Rounding a nearby bend, he sighted his quarry, a dark moving blotch against the gray of the trail. They still kept to their leisurely pace but rode purposefully, evidently having some definite objective in view. He eased Shadow's pace a little, until the group was barely discernible in the starlight and felt confident that he would not in turn be detected.

For quite a few miles the slow stalk continued. Then

abruptly the six turned to the left and vanished from sight; evidently they were following a fork of the trail that led up the slope from the Valley to the prairie beyond. Slade quickened Shadow's pace and soon reached the point where the trail branched.

Now it was very dark beneath the growth that bristled up close to the trail and sometimes overhung it with interlaced branches. But Slade was confident that the horsemen would keep to the trail and rode steadily, although now he could see nothing ahead.

Several more miles and the trail developed an upward slant; it was beginning to climb the Valley slope, which here was quite gradual and easy to negotiate.

Gradually the rise grew steeper and Slade knew he must be nearing the lip of the Valley. He slowed a little and his vigilance increased.

Abruptly the growth thinned and the crest of the rise loomed against the sky; there was no one in sight. He quickened Shadow's gait until he was but a hundred yards or so below the lip, then slowed him. He was sure that on the level prairie he would be able to see the group once more, and wanted to be equally sure they would not spot him at the same time, which they might conceivably do if they had happened to slow down for some reason or other.

Another moment and he reached the crest and the treeless rangeland lay before him. And as he had anticipated, far ahead was the moving blotch. He halted Shadow for a few moments, carefully surveying the terrain in every direction, against the possibility that the group ahead might be expecting reinforcements.

If so, they were nowhere in sight, so he rode on, following that faint and formless shadow that nevertheless could not be mistaken because of its steady forward movement.

West by slightly south the route led, onto what was now owned rangeland; several times he passed clumps of grazing cattle that eyed the lone horseman dubiously for a moment, then turned back to the grass.

As they continued on and on, Slade began to wonder where the devil the bunch was headed for. He knew that they were no great distance from the New Mexico state line. Perhaps they were keeping an appointment with some outlaw bunch in the wild land beyond. That could be it, although he thought it unlikely.

Suddenly the moving shadow swerved and flowed directly south, toward where another shadow, a stationary shadow, loomed darkly. Which Slade quickly recognized as one of the infrequent stands of chaparral that bristled up from the prairie like a cluster of flung spears. He turned likewise, slantingly, his eyes fixed on the horsemen. They drew nearer the growth, which a few minutes later swallowed them in its dark depths.

Now *El Halcón* found himself confronted by something of a dilemma. If he rode up to the brush and the hellions happened to be holed up there watching their back trail, he would be a settin' quail. He halted Shadow for a moment and considered. Arriving at a decision, he, too, rode south, but by slightly west, on a long diagonal that would bring him to the east end of the belt of growth but quite a bit south of its northern edge. That way he would be less liable to detection as he drew near the brush.

Just the same, it was an uneasy business, riding across the star-lit prairie. For all he knew the bunch of dubious characters might have turned east after they entered the chaparral and were even now approaching its eastern terminus.

If so, quite likely the first warning he would have of their presence would be the flash of a gun, the report of which he would not hear.

He breathed easier and his pulses slowed a bit as he reached the edge of the growth with nothing happening. He pulled up to consider a moment, then rode south along its straggle, keeping in the shadow as much as possible.

Finally he reached the south end of the belt, rode on a few paces and paused.

Directly opposite from where the riders had entered the growth and some four or five hundred yards to the south was a dark mass that he instantly catalogued as a fairly large herd of cattle. He could just make out the shadowy forms of two nighthawks riding slowly around the herd.

And as his gaze swept toward the brush he saw something else. There were no horses in sight, but creeping along toward the herd and at least seven hundred yards from where he sat his mount, were almost indiscernible shapes. Even at that distance, his keen vision caught the flash of starlight on metal.

The six riders, rifles in hand, were slowly approaching the sleeping herd and the unwary guards.

Now their objective was plain. A widelooping was in the making. Their intention was to grab the herd and run it across the New Mexico line, to where there was a ready sale for purloined cows.

But that wasn't all, and not what concerned the Ranger most. Snake-blooded murder was also in the making.

Slade knew he would have to act fast were he to save the two nighthawks. As soon as the killers got within good shooting distance, they would both die, in the true Sosna fashion. There was but one thing to do; the hellions were not far from a thousand yards distant, and they were on the ground while he was mounted. A frightful risk to take. He did not hesitate. His great voice rang out—

"Trail, Shadow, trail!"

Instantly the tall horse lunged forward, gathering speed with every beat of his flying hoofs. Slade drew his Winchester from the saddle boot, leaned far forward, his eyes never leaving the creeping shapes.

It was inevitable that they would spot him, and quickly. But that would take their attention from the unconscious cowboys who rode their monotonous chore under the stars.

Things worked out just as he expected. He saw the sudden convulsive movement of the vague shapes as the wideloopers spun about to face the approaching horseman. Then a flash of flame. A bullet whined by, close. Another followed and another. Slade bent low in the saddle, estimated the distance. Shadow had cut the near a thousand yards to less than six hundred.

Bullets were buzzing past like angry hornets, but Slade risked another fifty yards before pulling back hard on the reins. As Shadow slowed, he left the saddle in a streaking dive, landing on his hands and knees. Again his voice rang out—

"In the clear, feller!"

Shadow instantly whirled about and raced toward the growth, out of the line of fire.

A slug fanned Slade's face as he clamped the Winchester to his shoulder. His eyes glanced along the sights. The rifle bucked and spurted flame and smoke.

One of the crouching owlhoots leaped into the air, hands

clutching for the stars, and pitched forward onto his face. Slade fired again, and thought he saw a second man roll sideways, but couldn't be sure that his bullet had taken effect. Now the orange flashes were gushing toward him in a steady stream. A slug whipped through the crown of his hat. Another kicked dirt into his face and almost blinded him for an instant. He lunged forward and stretched out prone on the ground, the rifle stock cuddled against his cheek. The odds were darned lopsided and it was only a matter of time until the devils found the range. But help was on the way.

The two nighthawks had been utterly bewildered by the suddenness of the uproar which shattered the peaceful silence of the night. But only for a moment. Quickly they realized what was going on and were racing their horses toward the crouching outlaws, shooting and yelling.

Now guns were going off in every direction. The silence had given place to a hideous pandemonium of booming reports, yells, screams, curses, and the bawling of the terrified cows. It was a wild battle of shadowy shapes like demons risen from the Pit.

Three of the outlaws were down. The remaining trio leaped to their feet and fled madly for the shelter of the brush. The muzzle of Slade's rifle followed one and when it spurted flame, the devil went end over end like a plugged rabbit.

And like forty hen hawks on a setting quail, the cowboys swooped down on the remaining pair. The owlhoots turned and fought back with the desperation of despair, and went down with their guns flaming.

Slade whistled Shadow, who trotted forward, snorting disgustedly. Then he stood up and waved his hand, hoping the excitement-drunk punchers wouldn't throw down on him, too.

They didn't. They waved back and shouted. After pausing to make sure the outlaws were dead, they raced their horses toward him, jerked them to a slithering halt and dismounted. One strode forward, hand out-stretched. Even in the starlight his freckles were visible and he appeared hardly out of his teens; but he had a keen, alert look about him.

"Blazes, feller, where did you come from at just the right time?" he exclaimed shaking Slade's hand vigorously. "We didn't know what to make of it when you came skalleyhootin' across the range, but when we saw those snakes-in-the-grass throwing lead at you, we tumbled mighty fast. Knew *they*

67

weren't up to any good and figured we'd better join the party."

"I'm glad you caught on fast," Slade told him. "Things were getting a mite warm."

"Reckon they were, but I've a notion you'd have downed all the sidewinders without our help," the young cowboy declared admiringly. "The way you knocked off a couple was something. And the other one! He was streaking it for the brush like a coyote with its tail a-fire, but didn't do him any good. *That* was shooting!" He chortled with unholy glee at the recollection.

Immediately, however, he was grave, and his voice was a trifle strained when he resumed speaking.

"Guess we owe our hides to you, feller," he said. "Would have been just like when the Cartwright herd was run off last month. Three fellers were night guarding that herd and they never had a chance. When they found what was left of them, their irons were still in their holsters, and not a single cartridge had been busted. My name's Echols, Joyce Echols, and this old coot here who's doing all the talking is Cale Fenton. Let's have that lunch hook again."

Slade supplied his own name and the hand-shaking ceremony was repeated. The silent Fenton bobbed and grinned and said, "Much obliged!" But the way he said it packed plenty of weight.

"We ride for Keith Norman's XT," Joyce continued. "The Old Man will sure want to thank you for saving his cows and our worthless carcasses. He'd hate to lose us—keeps us on as horrible examples of what a cowhand hadn't ought to be. Fine old jigger. You can stick around and ride to the ranch-house, can't you? We'll get our relief in another hour or so."

"Guess I could do worse," Slade conceded.

"Fine!" Echols said. Fenton nodded vigorous agreement.

"See the cows have quieted," Joyce added. "A wonder they didn't stampede all over the lot. Guess they were too scared to run. So suppose we give those carcasses a once-over to make sure they've all gone to have a supper of hot coals with the Devil. Wait a minute, though, we got a lantern over by the herd; I'll fetch it."

He mounted and rode toward the cattle, that had settled down to chewing their cuds once more, singing softly in a high, sweet voice to soothe their nerves. He was back shortly

68

with the lantern and by its light they examined the bodies of the dead outlaws.

"Ornery looking specimens," Echols remarked. "Look like they've got some Indian blood or something like it."

Slade did not comment but he was pretty sure that they had been some of Sosna's Comancheros, all right. A pity the outlaw leader didn't come along on the raid.

Methodically he turned out the dead men's pockets but revealed nothing of note save a large sum of money.

"That dinero should go to you," Joyce declared. "You sure earned it. If you don't take it, Sheriff Davenport will sock it in the county treasury."

Slade smilingly shook his head. "Fact is," he said, blandly, as he stood up and turned around, "fact is I don't recall seeing any money. But I do think that fellows who take good care of a shipping herd deserve a nice celebration in town every now and then. I'm going to try and locate the horses."

As he walked away he heard chuckles behind him.

ELEVEN

THE OUTLAWS' HORSES he located without difficulty, good looking and docile animals tethered to branches. He released and led them back to the waiting cowboys. The money was nowhere in sight, but the outlaws' rifles had been neatly stacked, the bodies laid out in an orderly row.

"When we reach the ranchhouse, have your boss send word to Sheriff Davenport of what happened," he told the punchers. "He'll want to ride over and have a look."

"We'll do that," Echols promised. "Let's get back to the cows and make ready to ride. Boys should be here any minute now."

While they waited for the relief to arrive, Slade gave the herd a once-over and commented on the excellence of the cows.

"See your boss goes in for improved stock," he remarked.

"That's right," agreed Echols. "He says folks are asking for better beef than the longhorns can hand out and to hold your market you better give them what they want."

"He evidently is a man of progressive ideas, and he is right," Slade said. "Better beef, better prices and a larger percentage of profit."

"I can see that," answered the alert young Echols. "If I ever get into business myself, and I hope to, I'll sure keep it in mind. This is part of a shipping herd we're getting together. Already contracted for, and at top prices. Hey! here come the boys who'll sing to 'em till daylight. Now we can go."

Two young rannies rode up to the herd. "Everything okay?" one asked, glancing questioningly at Slade.

"Everything hunky-dory," Echols replied, " 'cept we killed a few skunks we found crawling around in the grass."

The two punchers looked slightly puzzled and stared at him.

"Stay in your hulls a minute, and I'll show you the pelts," Echols said, forking his own mount.

"Joyce just has to make a joke whenever he gets a chance," Fenton chuckled. "Never forget the time he coiled up a dead snake in the range Boss's blankets. Only trouble was, the snake wasn't as dead as he thought it was and scared Bolivar, the range boss, into tryin' to pray. But all he could remember was, 'Now I lay me! Now I lay me!' Listen, they've got there."

A storm of profanity and bellowed questions shattered the silence of the night. A moment later the three cowboys came dashing back. The new arrivals dismounted and shook hands with Slade.

"Much obliged, feller," they said in chorus. *"Muchas gracias!"*

"We're taking him to the Old Man," Echols announced. "Be seeing you. Guess you might as well get the rigs off those horses; they'll be more comfortable. Don't reckon anything else will happen tonight, but keep your eyes skun. Come on, Slade, let's go."

Slade mounted Shadow and they headed due west, splashing through a small stream that was the reason for the herd being held where it was. Less than two miles of riding and they sighted a big gray ranchhouse set in a grove of old trees.

70

"It's late, but I reckon we'd better wake up the Old Man and tell him what happened," Echols decided.

Repeated hammering on the front door caused a light to flash up. The door was opened, revealing a big old man, barefooted and clad in a long robe. He had gray hair and a questioning eye.

"Now what?" he demanded in a rumbling voice. "Drunk again, I suppose."

"Boss, we got something to tell you," Echols replied.

"Come in and shut the door," old Keith Norman invited. Echols added, "Boss, this is Slade. I figure you'll be glad to know him."

Norman extended a gnarled hand and there was the suspicion of a twinkle in his frosty eyes.

"How are you, Slade?" he asked. "Sorry to see you in such bad company, but they took me in, too, some years back. What you got to tell me, Joyce?"

The story came out with a rush, and the part Slade played lost nothing in the telling. Old Keith shook hands again.

"Puts me sorta heavy in your debt, son," he said to Slade. "I won't forget it. Fenton, hustle to the bunkhouse and tell Bolivar to send somebody for Sheriff Davenport, then put up the horses and come back. Bring Slade's saddle pouches in; he'll sleep here. Come on to the kitchen, Slade. You, too, Joyce, and I'll rustle some hot coffee and a snack. Won't bother to wake the cook just yet; he's old and needs his rest."

Slade walked out with Fenton and introduced him to Shadow. He secured his saddle pouches and returned to the ranchhouse.

Echols shook up the banked fire and put on fresh fuel. Old Keith got busy with pots and skillets. While he was cooking, Fenton returned.

"Bolivar sent Jed to tell the sheriff what happened," he said to Norman. "Wouldn't be surprised if he makes it here by sometime this afternoon, if Jed finds him in."

"Waste of time," grunted Norman. "Best to leave those varmints where they are to pizen the coyotes and the buzzards. More wood on the fire, Joyce."

Soon they sat down to a tasty snack and steaming coffee, of which all partook with appreciation.

While they were eating, the cook, an old Mexican, put in

71

an appearance. He started, stared at Slade, then bowed his head reverently. Slade voiced a greeting in flawless Spanish, to which the old fellow, smilingly delightedly, replied in kind, and got busy preparing breakfast for the hands.

Keith Norman glanced from one to the other with a puzzled expression, but did not comment.

After they finished eating, Echols and Fenton toddled off to the bunkhouse and some sleep. Slade and Norman, vacating the dining room for the hands who would soon be trooping in for breakfast, repaired to the big living room, which was tastefully furnished, boasting among other things, a grand piano which caught Slade's eyes; he wondered who played.

The cook brought them cups of coffee, which, with a low bow to Slade, he placed on a convenient table. Norman evidently noted the bow, but said nothing.

Rolling a cigarette, Slade sat back comfortably in an easy chair, a cup of coffee at his elbow. Old Keith hauled out a black pipe and loaded it.

For some minutes they sipped coffee and smoked in silence. Then Norman spoke.

"How'd you catch on to what those hellions had in mind, son?" he asked.

Slade studied him for a moment before replying. He thought he appeared intelligent and, he judged, was trustworthy. He decided to take him into his confidence, to an extent.

"Ever hear of Veck Sosna?" he asked.

"Why, sure," Norman replied. "The Comanchero outlaw who raised the devil hereabouts a few years ago. I heard tell he's back."

"He's back, all right," Slade said, a trifle grimly. "And raising the devil again, too. So far that I know of, he's robbed a stage, wrecked a train and tried to rob an Amarillo saloon. Would appear now that he's turning to cattle."

Norman stared. "You mean it was some of his devils who tried to wideloop my cows?"

"They were," Slade answered. "I'd been trailing them from the Canadian Valley, wondering what they had in mind."

Old Keith suddenly sat bolt upright in his chair, staring at Slade.

"Well, I'll be darned!" he rumbled. "No wonder old Pedro,

72

the cook, stood up on his toes when he sighted you. Son, you're *El Halcón*! Right?"

"I've been called that," Slade admitted. Old Keith whistled.

"Johnny Davenport was talking to me about you!" he exclaimed. "Said you were a right hombre and not to let anybody tell me different. Guess Johnny knew what he was talking about."

"I hope so," Slade smiled.

"Johnny don't make many mistakes," Norman declared. "Well, if this don't take the hide off the barn door! He told me how you've been chasin' Sosna all over Texas. Gather you ain't over fond of the sidewinder."

"Well, he's tried to kill me a few times," Slade equivocated. Norman nodded his understanding.

"That does cause a feller to sort of get his bristles up a mite," he conceded. "Well, here's hoping you get the horned toad leaning against the hot end of a passing slug. The sooner the better for everybody concerned. From all I can gather, he's vicious as a Gila monster like they have over in Arizona, and ornery as a hyderphobia skunk."

"Yes, he's all of that," Slade agreed. Old Keith suddenly chuckled.

"I was thinking about what Johnny Davenport said about you," he explained. " 'The singingest man in the whole Southwest, with the fastest gunhand!' "

"I fear Johnny is prone to exaggeration," Slade replied with a smile.

"Can't say as to the singing part, but from what Joyce Echols said about the way you clipped those three hellions you throwed down on, I've a notion he didn't stretch a point when it comes to the gun slinging," Norman declared. "Said he never saw such shootin', and by starlight, too."

"Light wasn't too bad, and the distance not too great," Slade deprecated the feat.

"Uh-huh, only better'n five hundred yards," Norman commented dryly.

"And I gather they were squattin' on the ground," he added. "Which helped, of course."

Slade laughed, and dropped the subject. Norman studied him in turn, seemed to hesitate. Then—

"Son, I know how you feel about Sosna," he said slowly,

73

"but don't you think it would be better to leave him to the authorities to deal with? That's their chore. And I'm telling you, the grudge trail ain't a nice one to follow and there ain't much satisfaction to be tied onto at the end of it. I know something about that. Followed one myself once, when I was about your age. Figured I was justified in doing so. Came out on top, but I never felt over good about it."

"I wouldn't argue that point with you, sir," Slade replied gravely.

Old Keith nodded vigorously. "So I think it would be better for a fine young feller like you to stop mavierickin' around looking for trouble and settle down," he said. "If you hanker for a chore of riding in a good section, there's one right here for you to tie onto. And Ted Bolivar, my range boss, won't be with me much longer—figures to branch out on his own —and none of my other work dodgers are up to the chore. What do you say?"

Slade opened his lips to reply, then closed them again, his eyes fixed on the stairway that led to the second story of the ranchhouse.

A girl was tripping down the stairs. She wasn't very tall, but her proportions were guaranteed to catch the masculine eye, and hold it. Her little heart-shaped face, Slade thought elfinly beautiful, with its great dark eyes and very red lips. Her hair also was dark and inclined to curl.

"Good morning, Uncle Keith," she said in a soft low voice.

"Mornin', Jerry," Norman answered. "This here is Walt Slade, a young feller who did me a mighty good turn last night. Slade, she's my niece, Jerry Norman."

"Short for Geraldine, Mr. Slade," the girl explained, extending a little sun-golden hand over which Slade bowed gracefully.

"I was just trying to get him to sign up with us," Norman broke in.

"Well," Slade said, smiling broadly, "the offer certainly has attractions."

Miss Norman evidently understood, for she laughed with a flash of little white teeth, and the color in her creamily tanned cheeks rose a little.

"I hope you'll see fit to accept the offer, Mr. Slade," she said.

"I'll consider it very seriously," he promised.

74

"And now, son," said old Keith, "it's time we put you to bed. You had a hard night and you look tired. Jerry, show him to the guest room."

Securing his saddle pouches, Slade followed her up the stairs. She opened a door to reveal a neatly furnished room that boasted two windows and a wide bed.

"I hope you'll be comfortable, Mr. Slade," she said.

"I'm sure I will be, *Miss* Norman," he replied, smiling down at her from his great height.

As before, she was quick to understand, and smiled and dimpled.

"Sleep as long as you wish to," she said. "Your breakfast will be ready whenever you choose to get up. So goodnight, or good morning—Walt."

"Thank you—Jerry," he answered. She glanced over her shoulder as she closed the door, and pattered down the stairs.

Slade did not immediately go to sleep after he stretched out on the very comfortable bed. He did take time to seriously consider Keith Norman's offer. Might be a very good idea to take him up on it, for a while. He had a hunch that Sosna might well visit reprisals on the XT ranch. He would undoubtedly be in a towering rage when he heard of the fatal miscarriage of his plans. And if he learned *El Halcón* was riding for Norman that would be an added incentive. Which could possibly bring the outlaw leader to him. So before he went to sleep, he concluded to accept the offer.

As to whether big dark eyes and red lips had any bearing on his decision was problematical and he did not discuss it with himself, at least not audibly.

TWELVE

DOWNSTAIRS, JERRY NORMAN turned to her uncle. "Whe-e-ew!" she exclaimed. "Where did *he* come from?"

There was a twinkle in old Keith's eyes when he replied,

75

"From most everywhere, I guess; that's *El Halcón,* the notorious outlaw."

His niece stared at him. "Well," she said, "you can call it a woman's intuition if you wish, but I'm of the opinion we could do with quite a few *outlaws* of his kind."

"Amen!" old Keith seconded vigorously. "Sit down, chick, and I'll tell you what he did."

Keith Norman knew how to tell a story and Jerry pressed one hand hard against her mouth, her eyes wide, as he vividly described the crawling outlaws with rifles ready for the kill.

"And if it wasn't for him the boys would have been murdered," she said when he paused. "Joyce Echols, who's like a brother to me. And Cale Fenton, who's like another uncle. I —I could—kiss him!"

"Better be careful, you'll scare him," old Keith warned.

Miss Norman sniffed. "*Him* scared of a woman! But," she added thoughtfully, "the woman might find herself scared— of herself."

Her uncle looked puzzled, but she did not elaborate.

Relaxed and complacent because of the successful culmination of the night's stirring happenings, Slade slept soundly until awakened by afternoon sunshine streaming through the window. For a few minutes he lay further considering Keith Norman's offer of a chore of riding, and reaffirmed his decision to accept the offer.

First, though, he would ride to Amarillo for a consultation with Sheriff Brian Carter. The matter brought to a satisfactory conclusion in his mind, he arose, washed up and descended to the living room, where he found Jerry Norman curled up in an easy chair.

"Hello?" she greeted. "Ready for breakfast?"

"Guess I could stand a bite," he admitted.

She bounced out of the chair. "I'll tell Pedro to rattle his hocks as Uncle Keith would say," she replied. "I'll have coffee with you."

"That makes the prospect of breakfast even more alluring," he said, with a smile.

"Sounds flattering anyhow," she laughed.

"Definitely not," he differed. "Flattery presupposes an attempt to ingratiate oneself. My remark was a precise statement of fact."

76

A little pucker showed between her delicate black brows as she regarded him.

"Your choice of words is somewhat unusual—for a cowhand," she commented.

"Possibly, for—a cowhand," he smilingly agreed. Jerry shook her curly head and hurried to the kitchen, where a rattling of pots and skillets immediately sounded.

Jerry returned shortly, plumped into a chair, crossed very shapely legs and again regarded him steadfastly for a few moments.

"Well," she said at length, "going to sign up with us?"

"I think I shall, after I return from Amarillo," he replied.

"You're not going to ride there today?"

"No, not today," he answered. "Sheriff Davenport will desire that I be here when he arrives. I'll ride first thing in the morning."

"I wish," she said slowly, "that you would sign up before you leave."

"Why?"

"Because then, as half owner of the spread, I could give you an order and make it stick."

Slade shook with laughter. Somehow the way she put it struck him as being highly amusing. She regarded him with disapproval.

"I don't see anything funny about it," she insisted.

"What would be the order?" he countered.

"That you allow me to ride with you; I'd like to do some shopping in Amarillo."

"An order is not necessary to cause me to grant a request that would give me great personal pleasure," he said. "But you'd have to stay overnight in Amarillo. I don't expect to ride back this way until the following day."

"I've stayed overnight there before," she replied blithely. "Then it's all settled?"

"So far as I am concerned," he said. "But how about your uncle? He may object to trusting you to the hands of one who is practically a stranger to you both."

"After the way he sang your praises this morning? I believe he'd even trust his pet saddle horse to you."

Slade laughed again; she was certainly a refreshing little body.

"And how about you?" he asked.

Her eyes crinkled a little at the corners. "I think you have very nice hands," she replied.

"Come along," she added, jumping to her feet. "There's Pedro calling you to breakfast. And the things *he* said about you!"

"Not too derogatory, I hope."

"Derogatory! They would have made an ivory statue blush with pleasure."

"I am not sure I'm complimented by the comparison," he laughed. "Ivory is cold and lifeless."

"Galatea was an ivory statue, but she came to life," Jerry said softly.

"At Pygmalion's touch."

She blushed a little when she replied, but the big dark eyes met his squarely.

"Could not the reverse be true?"

"Without a doubt!" he concurred with a heartiness that caused the blush to heighten.

Pedro called again and they hurried to the dining room where the old cook had outdone himself in deference to the honored guest.

"You inspire him," Jerry laughed, and quoted softly, " '*El Halcón*! the just, the good, the friend of the lowly!' And I believe every word he said."

"Thank you," Slade said simply. "I hope I'll never disillusion you."

"Oh, you'll never disillusion me, for I have no illusions where you are concerned. I understand what you are and how you are made; and can be content with the crumbs that 'fall from the table'! Pedro has inspired *me*; although I shouldn't so soon after breakfast, I'll eat with you," she added gaily, relieving the wistful somberness of her previous remark. "Goodness! don't put such a tremendous helping on my plate! I have to watch my figure, you know."

"Spare yourself the effort, it's being watched, quite closely," he replied with an emphasis that caused the roses to really bloom in her cheeks.

They had a very pleasant breakfast together, after which they returned to the living room, where Slade sat smoking in silence for a while and Jerry watched him, also in silence, which he eventually broke.

78

"I believe you said you are half owner of the spread?" he remarked, interrogatively.

"That's right," she replied. "Dad and Uncle Keith were partners, and when Dad died, five years ago, I inherited his share. Don't let it bother you. Uncle Keith handles the spread, so you won't be working for a woman boss, something many cowhands object to."

"I'm not afflicted by that particular idiosyncrasy," he denied smilingly. "And, after all, doesn't a man usually end up, sooner or later, taking orders from a woman?"

Jerry shrugged daintily. "Not in your case, I fear," she said. "I doubt if you'll ever take orders from a woman."

"Will depend on circumstances and conditions," he answered, still smiling. Jerry lowered her dark lashes.

Sheriff Davenport arrived soon afterward, with him a deputy driving a light wagon. He said hello to Jerry, shook hands warmly with Slade.

"So, see you're still collecting bodies," he remarked. "Nice of you to divide up the business between Brian Carter and me; wouldn't want you to play favorites. Suppose you tell me just what happened. Jed, who brought me the word, was sorta vague."

Slade told him, tersely and to the point. The old sheriff nodded from time to time and tugged his mustache.

"A good chore," he said when the tale was finished. "So it's Sosna back, all right. I had the right notion when I told you he'd be liable to be hanging around Amarillo. Pity you didn't bag him along with the others. He's a hellion. I'd hoped when you chased him away from here a few years back that we'd seen the last of him. Well, his sashay up here may prove to be his big mistake."

"Possibly," Slade conceded. "Looks like his luck should run out sometime. The trouble is, though, luck plays but a minor role in his operations. It's his shrewdness and hairtrigger reactions that save him."

"Only a matter of time," Davenport declared. "My money's on *El Halcón*. And now," he continued, "if you'll lead the way we'll pick up those carcasses and pack them in the wagon. Still got plenty of daylight, I figure."

"Only a couple of miles to go," Slade replied. "I'll get my horse."

"You're spending the night, of course, Sheriff," Jerry said.

"If it won't inconvenience you," Davenport answered.

"We have plenty of room," she assured him. "I'll go with you to get your horse, Walt. I looked in on him this morning; what a beauty!"

"He'll do," Slade replied. "Let's go."

As they entered the stable, he said, "If you're short of room, the sheriff or the deputy can have mine; I'll sleep under a tree. I'm used to it."

She smiled a little, blushed a little, and replied,

"I don't think that would be—necessary."

He chuckled, cupped his hands around her slender waist and lifted her until her face was on a level with his. Their lips clung together before he dropped her back on her feet.

Her big eyes were a trifle misty, but she laughed gaily—

"A crumb from the rich man's table! My remark at breakfast was prophetic."

Before he could frame an adequate retort, she was across the stable to the stalls, talking to Shadow, who regarded her with distinct approval.

When they reached the scene of the widelooping attempt, Sheriff Davenport took one look at the dead outlaws and nodded vigorously.

"Yep, Comancheros, all right," he said. "Still quite a few of the hellions up around the Oklahoma Border and over in the Cap Rock hills. Ornery devils! Okay, Pres, into the wagon with 'em and cover 'em with the blankets. They'll keep till we get 'em to Tascosa.

"Nope, you don't need to attend the inquest if you ain't of a mind to," he answered Slade's question. "Echols and Fenton will be enough. If necessary, I'll just say I couldn't find you. Be nothing but a formality, anyhow. All right, let's get going; I'm hungry."

At suppertime Slade met the rest of the XT hands and liked them. They were mostly fresh-faced young rannies typical of the rangeland; but a few, including Fenton and Bolivar, the range boss, were middle-aged men who had been with Keith Norman for years.

After supper was over, the young hands trooped off to the bunkhouse and a poker game. Fenton, Bolivar and one or two others repaired to the sitting room to exchange reminiscences with Sheriff Davenport, who was an old friend. Later, at her uncle's request, Jerry played the piano for them, very nicely, Slade thought.

Sheriff Davenport's eyes twinkled as he listened and when she left the stool he said to Slade,

"All right, Walt, now let's hear what the singingest man in the whole Southwest can do."

Jerry's eyes widened. "Can he sing?" she asked.

"Wait!" chuckled the sheriff. "Go ahead, Walt."

Slade sat down at the piano and ran his slender fingers over the keys with a master's touch. Then in deference to the cowhands, he threw back his black head and sang a rollicking ballad of the range:—

> Oh, I'm a lonesome gamblin' man;
> If my horse he don't go lame,
> I'm ridin' down to Silvertown
> To gamble my last game!
> I'm ridin' down to Silvertown
> To buy a stack of blues;
> With my honey-gal a-waitin' here,
> Why, pardner, I can't lose!
> I'm goin' to play 'em wide and high
> At every place in town,
> And when I've busted every bank
> I aims to settle down.
> Oh, I'm a lonesome gamblin' man
> With a derringer in my sleeve!
> If I don't come ridin' back again,
> Why, Honey, don't you grieve!

And as the great golden, metallic baritone-bass pealed and thundered through the room, the entranced listeners could vision the gay and carefree horseman in his long black coat, his flowered satin vest and his snowy, ruffled shirt front riding blithely to his rendezvous with death.

The music ended with a crash of chords and was followed by cries for another.

"Please do, Walt!" Jerry urged. So he turned laughing eyes to her, and sang—

> Little whispers in the night,
> Drowsy murmurs sweet—

81

Were they silenced by the miles,
Were the world complete?
But oh, the wind upon the trail!
And the dust of gypsy feet!

Jerry didn't laugh. Her eyes were misty, and she sighed.
Later, when they were along in the living room, she said,
"Yes, the wind and the dust and the gypsy trail! I fear they
are stronger than whispers in the night."

"Whispers can be sweet."

"Yes. And a wonderful memory, at least."

THIRTEEN

WHEN JERRY appeared ready to ride the following morning,
Slade's eyes mirrored approval of her costume. She was
dressed in Levi's, the bibless overalls favored by the cowhands, that showed signs of plenty of wear, scuffed little
boots, a soft blue shirt, open at the throat, and a neatly
creased J.B. perched jauntily on her dark curls.

"Perfect!" he said. "I was afraid you'd come down in a
modish riding costume."

"Not a chance," she laughed. "I was brought up on the
range, remember. I have a dress, and some other things, in
my saddle pouch, though. You'll have to take me to dinner
tonight and I wouldn't want to look like a hoyden."

"Impossible!" he declared. "As I told you last night, you
look wonderful in anything, or—"

She reached up and put a pink palm firmly across his lips.
"You're not *whispering* now," she reminded him.

Slade laughed and his gaze centered on the serviceable
looking gun swung at her hip.

"Oh, I can shoot," she said. "And you never can tell, it
might come in handy."

Walt Slade was to remember that remark, later.

82

It was midmorning when they left the ranchhouse, after telling Sheriff Davenport goodbye, he and his deputy and his wagonload of bodies setting out much earlier, accompanied by Fenton and Joyce Echols.

They had a long ride ahead of them but Slade figured they should reach Amarillo by late afternoon.

However, after they had covered a few miles, Jerry had a suggestion to make.

"Walt," she said, "would you mind very much if we rode by way of the Valley trail? I love the Valley, it is so beautiful at this time of the year, so different from the flat and treeless prairie."

Slade hesitated. The Canadian Valley *was* beautiful, but some of the things it harbored were not. But really there should be no danger in broad daylight.

"It's the longer route and we'll be late getting to town," he pointed out.

"Who cares!" she countered blithely. "Come on!"

"Okay," he replied, and turned Shadow's head north.

They experienced little difficulty descending into the Valley and after a while reached the trail which ran close to the river, the trail, incidentally, that Slade had followed while stalking the wideloopers a few nights before.

Here the river was a limpid stream about twenty feet wide of clear water. Its banks were fringed with wild chokeberries, plums, wild gooseberries and grapes. There were many cottonwood mottes, or groves, scattered along the banks. A quite different terrain from the sun-baked prairie where at this time of the year even the grass looked hot.

"Isn't this a lot nicer?" Jerry asked. "So nice and peaceful."

"Yes, it is," Slade admitted, "but I've known it to be far from peaceful."

In fact, he was already regretting having been persuaded to take the lower trail. He had an uneasy feeling that they would have been better off on the open prairie, where they could see for many miles in every direction. It seemed absurd to think that they would run onto some of the Sosna bunch prowling around in the full blaze of noon, but the unpleasant presentiment not only persisted but increased in force. He studied every motte and thicket, was vigilant at each bend in the trail, carefully watched the movements of birds and little animals in the brush. Jerry seemed to sense and understand his preoccupation, for she was silent, her big eyes fixed on his face.

At times the trail ran arrow-straight for long distances, then it turned snake-in-a-cactus patch and twisted and turned. Quite often Slade could not see fifty yards ahead. Which did not tend to enhance his peace of mind.

The turns were bad enough, but the straight stretches were even worse, for then distance played into the hands of a possible drygulcher. He could remain concealed while they rode past his hiding place and then open fire within easy rifle range with little danger to himself. So Slade not only studied the terrain ahead but continually glanced over his shoulder for a possible faint movement in the brush that would betray the holed-up killer.

As a result, after negotiating a series of bends and then progressing for some six hundred yards on a straight stretch, he instantly spotted the four riders who bulged around the last turn and sped toward them.

For a moment he gazed, then faced to the front and spoke to his companion.

"Speed up," he said. "Get everything you can out of that crowbait. Get going, Shadow!"

Instantly the black horse lengthened his stride; the sturdy little bay the girl rode kept pace.

Slade glanced back again. The four riders were urging their horses to greater speed. He spoke to Shadow, and the race was on.

Very quickly, however, *El Halcón* realized it was a losing race so far as they were concerned. The bay, though sturdy, was no speed horse and the sinister quartet was closing the distance. Even as he glanced back, a puff of smoke mushroomed from their ranks. A slug whined past.

Slade went cold all over. Bitterly he cursed his folly that exposed the girl to such danger. Better she be killed outright, though, than to fall into the hands of those sadistic devils. His face set in granite lines, his eyes were cold as the waters of a glacial lake.

"Listen," he told Jerry. "From now on, do exactly what I tell you. Don't hesitate. I'm afraid we are up against a showdown. If anything happens to me, use that gun of yours on the

84

hellions for five cartridges. Save the sixth and last for yourself. Do you understand?"

"I understand, and I'll do just as you say," she replied quietly. He shot her a glance of admiration. Her face was pale, her eyes wide, but she showed no signs of hysterics or panic."

"Good girl!" he said, and was rewarded by a wan smile.

Another bullet sang by, closer, and another. Slade's mind worked at hairtrigger speed. Should they turn into the brush and hope to escape under cover of the chaparral? Wouldn't work.

Again the problem was the slow-paced bay. Pluck her from the saddle and trust to Shadow's great speed and endurance to see them through? He shook his head. The pursuit was exceedingly well mounted—trust Sosna to procure only the best for his devils. The added weight would be too great a handicap for the black horse. Hole up in the growth and shoot it out with the hellions? Still not too good. There might well be more of them around that would be attracted by the gunfire. He resolved on a more daring plan, one that might meet with success. Worth trying, anyhow, for as it was they were on the losing end of the string. The bend ahead was now only a couple of hundred yards distant. If they could just make it to that before a slug found its mark! The pursuit was still nearly four hundred yards to the rear.

They made it! Unharmed, they swerved around the bend and out of sight of the pursuit. A dozen yards or so and Slade spoke to Shadow,

"Hold it!" He reached over, gripped the bay's bit iron and jerked it to a halt alongside Shadow.

"Unfork," he told his companion. "Lie flat on the ground behind me, at the edge of the brush."

Without question she obeyed. At his rider's word of command, Shadow dashed down the trail a few yards and into the brush, the bay following. Slade drew both guns and waited.

Around the bend careened the four pursuers. Slade opened fire the instant they showed, shooting with both hands. One man spun from the saddle. The others jerked their mounts to a slithering halt, shooting and yelling. Bullets stormed past the Ranger. He fired again, left and right. A second outlaw slumped forward and fell. A moment later a third

85

rose in his stirrups with a scream that crescendoed to a bubbling shriek and plunged to the ground, blood gushing from his bullet slashed throat.

And at the same instant, Slade's hat spun sideways on his head, the guns dropped from his nerveless hands and he fell forward on his face. The remaining outlaw gave a yell of triumph and lined sights with the prostrate Ranger.

Through a wave of blinding, pain-streaked light, Slade heard a gun crack behind him, and again.

Surrounded! was his last thought before utter blackness rolled down upon him, fold on clammy fold.

FOURTEEN

When Walt Slade recovered consciousness, his head was pillowed in Jerry's lap and she was bathing his forehead with a wet handkerchief. Sobs convulsed her slender form and tears streamed down her face. He gazed up at her blankly for a moment. She gave a glad little cry.

"Oh, my darling!" she sobbed. "Are you all right? I feared you were dead!"

"All right except for a headache," he mumbled, shaking that member vigorously to free his brain of cobwebs. "Lend me a hand."

With her help he managed a sitting position, still shaking his head. Mechanically he raised a hand to his throbbing forehead and discovered a sizeable lump just above his left temple.

"You've got an awful bruise but there doesn't seem to be any blood," Jerry said.

For a moment Slade was at a loss to understand what had happened to him. Then his glance fell on his hat that lay nearby. The heavy buckle which held the band in place was bent sideways and hanging by a thread.

"Of all the freakish things!" he exclaimed. "The slug hit

86

the buckle, slammed it against my head and knocked me out."

He glanced apprehensively up the trail. Four riderless horses stood there, gazing at him inquiringly. In the dust lay four motionless forms.

Jerry was clinging to him, shuddering convulsively.

"What's the matter?" he asked anxiously. "You hurt?"

"N-no," she faltered. "It's—it's just that I never—killed a man before!"

"And you didn't kill one this time," he reassured her. "You killed a beast. So it was your iron that went off behind me!"

"Yes," she said, adding simply. "I had to shoot him—he was going to kill you."

"Good girl!" he repeated his former remark. "Yes, you're a girl to ride the river with!"

She smiled wanly at the greatest compliment the rangeland can pay. Slade stood up, weaving a little on his feet. But he soon steadied and strode to the four patiently waiting horses. Working at top speed, he stripped off the rigs so the animals could drink and graze in comfort. The dead outlaws he spared but a passing glance; the sheriff could look after them.

Whistling Shadow, who came out of the brush and trotted to him, the bay ambling along behind, he turned to Jerry, picked her up and tossed her into the saddle and forked Shadow.

"We're getting out of here, fast," he said. "May be some more of the devils around somewhere."

As they rode down the trail at a good pace, Slade constantly scanned the growth on their right. Coming to a spot where it appeared sparse, he said, "turn south here and we'll make it up to the prairie. I've had enough of this snake hole for the present. All of a sudden, life very much in the open is attractive."

Threading their way through the chaparral, they reached the south wall of the Valley, which they negotiated without difficulty.

"This is better," Slade said, sweeping the level grassland with his gaze. "Now we've got more than one way to run."

"How are you feeling now, dear?" Jerry asked anxiously.

"Fine as frog hair," he replied. "Headache's all gone." He hauled off his bullet-torn hat as he spoke and patted it affectionately.

"Good old rainshed! If it hadn't been for that buckle which turned the slug, I'd likely have gotten really hurt."

"I want that buckle," Jerry said energetically. "I'm going to keep it forever. Give it to me and I'll buy you a new one."

With a chuckle, he jerked the buckle loose from the few threads that still held it in place and handed it to her. She kissed it and dropped it into her shirt pocket.

"What a waste of sweet lips!" he remonstrated.

"Well," she said, and sidled her horse closer.

"That's better," he said, a long moment later. "Now let's hightail to town before I topple over from starvation; gun fighting always makes me hungry."

"Me, too," was the ungrammatical response as she touched up the bay.

The sunset was flaming in scarlet and gold over distant Tucumcari mountain, which looks like the breasts of a sleeping woman, when they reached Amarillo without further mishap.

"There's a hotel on Tyler Street where I sleep when I happen to stay overnight in town," Jerry said. "If you'll take me there, I'll freshen up a bit before we eat."

"Okay," he replied. "While you're at it I'll put up the horses and drop in on Sheriff Carter for a few minutes."

The old room clerk smiled benignly on them when Slade registered for a room for her, but did not comment other than greeting her as an old friend. Slade chuckled. Jerry made a face at him and followed the clerk up the stairs.

Sheriff Carter was in his office when Slade arrived. Muttering profanity, he listened to the Ranger's recounting of the hectic experience in the Valley.

"I'll ride out there tomorrow and pick up the carcasses," he promised, adding in worried tones, "Blast it! they're after you hot and heavy. They're keeping tabs on every move you make."

"Well, it didn't do them much good this time, thanks to Jerry Norman," Slade pointed out.

"Uh-huh, Jerry's a fine gal, I knew her dad well, but you may not have a Jerry Norman with you next time. Okay, be seeing you."

When Slade reached the hotel, he found Jerry sitting in the lobby and wearing a dress that he thought very charming, especially with her inside it.

"Well, where do you want to eat?" he asked.

"Anywhere, just so there are lights and music and people talking and laughing," she replied.

"How about the rough and tough and salty Washout down by the lake?" he teased.

"That sounds wonderful," she enthused. "Let's go there."

"Didn't I tell you it's rough and tough and salty," he protested.

For the first time she mentioned, obliquely, the happening in the Valley. By tacit consent they had refrained from discussing it during their ride, Slade feeling that the quicker she forgot all about the bloody affair the better.

"Well, didn't I prove this afternoon that I can be a little salty myself?" she said.

"You sure did," he answered with emphasis. "If you hadn't been, the chances are I wouldn't be here right now."

"Let's don't talk about it," she said, her eyes darkening. "Take me to your rough and tough Washout."

Slade chuckled to himself as he realized that once again she had inveigled him into taking her on what might be considered a questionable venture. But there was no doubt that she had saved his life and he could hardly refuse her any request, even against his better judgment.

However, he had concluded in the course of his visits there, that the Washout was really not so black as Deputy Bill Harley had painted it. Rukuses now and then, perhaps, but the same applied to any place where men and women gathered to drink and enjoy themselves. The eminently respectable Trail End, he knew, had been the scene of more than one gun slinging. Like gold, trouble was where you found it, and it could come looking for you anywhere.

"I like this," Jerry giggled as they sauntered along the dimly lighted streets and listened to the raucous laughter drifting over the swinging doors. "Even if I don't look like one, according to you, I'm afraid I'm something of a hoyden at heart. Do you think I'm terrible, dear?"

"I think you're wonderful," he declared, and meant it.

"I'm glad you think so," she said, "especially after—after all!"

He smiled down at her. "You have a remarkable gift for saying nothing and at the same time saying a great deal," he observed.

89

"Well, darn it! didn't I say—enough?" she demanded, blushing a little.

"You certainly did, and beautifully. Just don't change."

"Huh! I won't change. I'll improve."

"Doesn't seem possible," he protested, "but perhaps what is demonstrated in practice will exceed what's set forth in precept."

"Now let me unscramble that one," she said. "Yes, I think I understand. You'll see! Say, isn't that your Washout you spoke of, across the street? That's what the lettering on the window says. Hurry, I'm famished."

There were a few stares when they entered the Washout, but nobody made a remark. The proprietor, fiercely mustached, keen-eyed and portly, escorted them to a table.

"Miss Norman, isn't it?" he said. "I remember seeing you with your uncle, who I've known for years. And Mr. Slade, of course; everybody knows *you*. Glad to have you both with us. Let me bring over a bottle of wine, on the house."

"I like him," Jerry whispered to Slade. "Guess you'll find nice people everywhere."

"Everywhere," the Ranger agreed. "No section has a monopoly on kindliness, courtesy and consideration."

"Do you know his name?" Jerry asked.

"I believe Bill Harley said it's Yates, Thankful Yates," Slade replied. "Has a New England sound, don't you think?"

Yates returned shortly. With a flourish, he poured golden wine into crystal goblets he had unearthed from somewhere.

"Made from Upper Rio Grande Valley grapes," he announced. "I don't think there's any better to be found anywhere in the world. Hope you'll like it."

"I'm sure we will, Mr. Yates, and thank you," Jerry said. Yates smiled happily and beckoned a waiter, who took their order.

Although it was still early, the Washout was already well crowded. The orchestra was busy scraping away. There were a number of couples on the dance floor. Both roulette wheels were spinning and there were several poker games in progress. Altogether, the scene was gay, animated and colorful.

Slade glanced at his pretty table companion and smiled. Her eyes were sparkling, her cheeks flushed, her red lips slightly parted. No doubt but that she was thoroughly enjoying herself. She caught his glance and smiled back.

90

"The kind of a place I've always wanted to visit," she said. "Uncle Keith always took me to what I suppose would be considered the more respectable places, and when Dad was alive, of course, I was too young. This I really like. The dance floor girls look nice."

"They are, in their own fashion," Slade conceded. Jerry shot him a look through her lashes.

"To each his own, or her own," she said. "I'm not throwing any rocks. Thank goodness! here comes our dinner. That wine just made me all the hungrier."

All the while Slade was closely watching the swinging doors, and not a man entered that he did not judge. He hadn't forgotten Sheriff Carter's warning. Very likely the old peace officer was right and that Sosna and his bunch were keeping tabs on his every movement, waiting for a chance to take him at a disadvantage. The happenings of the afternoon certainly pointed that way; he must have been under the scrutiny of malevolent eyes when he and Jerry descended to the Valley. A moment of carelessness might well prove disastrous.

Slade experienced a feeling that the long feud between him and Veck Sosna was drawing to a close. That here where the feud began it would end. The victor? Instinctively he shrugged his broad shoulders. Why seek to peer into the future, which from day to day would unroll itself as does a scroll? Be content with the present. Take what Fate gives of good or ill. With beauty beside him and laughter ringing in his ears, why pry and wonder? He raised his glass and drank a silent toast to the glory of the hour.

FIFTEEN

THEY LINGERED over their dinner, which they enjoyed with the appetite of youth and perfect health. Slade smoked a cigarette over a final cup of steaming coffee, while Jerry watched the dancers on the floor.

"Like to join them?" he asked.

"I'd love to," she replied. "Would it be all right?"

"Of course," he answered. "Let's go."

They had several dances, then returned to the table to relax a bit.

"You dance as you sing, wonderfully," Jerry declared a little breathlessly, "I sure enjoyed every moment. I've been cooped up so long. Tonight I'm really living, thanks to you."

"And tonight I also am really living, thanks to you," he replied with meaning.

Now the Washout was really hopping. The bar was crowded two-deep. Every available inch of the dance floor was occupied by shuffling couples. There were waiting lines at the roulette wheels and the faro bank. And everybody appeared to be having an uproarious good time.

Thankful Yates came across to their table, rubbing his hands together complacently.

"Where in blazes do they all come from?" he marvelled. "A bigger night than payday night. At this rate I'll be able to retire before I'm ninety. Enjoying yourself, folks? Fine! I'll send over another bottle of wine."

"We actually have finished the first one," Jerry giggled. "Oh, my poor complexion!"

"You needn't worry about it," Slade reassured her. "Besides, the wine, while it has a delightful bouquet and a mellow taste, is really not at all strong. That's one of the advantages of the Rio Grande grapes. Somehow they produce an excellent wine with a very low alcoholic content."

"Fortunate they do, otherwise I'd be falling over my own feet," Jerry declared. "It's nice and warming, too," she added, slanting him a glance through the silken curtain of her lashes.

"I don't think you need it," he replied, smiling, his eyes fixed on the swinging doors.

Yes, the Washout was really hopping . . . a perfect setup for trouble, quick and deadly.

An altercation started at the bar, near the door. Two men began shouting angrily at each other, waving their fists threateningly.

The place was in an uproar. Thankful Yates and his three floor men came plowing across the room. Everybody's attention was centered on the loudening row at the bar.

Not quite everybody's. Walt Slade's eyes never left the

swinging doors. He saw the three men bulge in and fan out apart. He was on his feet and in front of Jerry in a ripple of motion. His guns blazed before the attackers could pull trigger.

One man fell, kicking and thrashing. The other two, ducking, dodging, weaving, answered the Ranger shot for shot. Bullets thudded into the wall, hammered the swinging doors.

A second man pitched forward on his face to lie motionless. A slug slashed Slade's shirt sleeve. Another ripped through his already much abused hat which hung on a nail almost directly behind him. He fired left and right. The remaining killer slewed sideways and crumpled up. The whole deadly episode hadn't taken ten seconds.

Slade swept the room with his icy gaze. Men were shouting and cursing in bewilderment. The dance floor girls were shrieking. Thankful Yates was bellowing for order. But he could see no indications that anybody desired to horn in. Ejecting the spent shells from his guns and replacing them with fresh cartridges, he sat down and began rolling a cigarette with fingers that did not spill a crumb of tobacco. He smiled at Jerry, who was white to the lips.

"Why didn't I bring my gun along?" she wailed.

"Doubt if you'd had time to use it," Slade replied. "Things happened sort of fast."

"It *would* have looked a little out of place with a dress," she admitted, the feminine gaining the ascendancy. Slade chuckled and touched a match to his cigarette.

"How in the world did you know what those men intended?" she asked.

Slade shrugged. "An old trick, and sometimes it works," he said. "I've had it tried before. Start a row at the bar to attract everybody's attention. The killers slide in, do their work and are gone before anybody realizes what's happening. You see, I was watching the door. I knew that rukus was phony. Too much yelling and waving of arms."

The roses had returned to her cheeks, the scarlet to her mouth. She smiled, albeit a little tremulously.

"I'm learning," she said. "You're all right, aren't you, dear?"

"Nothing to complain about, except the damage done to my shirt and my rainshed. Look at it, will you?"

"I'm only glad it wasn't on your head," she replied, glancing toward the battered head gear. "Tomorrow I'm going to buy you a new one. Don't argue with me! I mean what I say."

Under the persuasive ministrations of Yates and his floor men, reinforced by two bartenders with sawed-off shotguns, order, or something resembling it, had been restored. Men gathered about the dead outlaws, staring at them, shifting their glances to Slade and shaking their heads.

"Some shooting!" was the almost universal remark.

Thankful Yates came lumbering across the room to the table. "Fine work, Mr. Slade, fine work!" he enthused. "You did for all three of 'em. One kicked a little, but he bled to death before I could club him. Fine work! I've sent for the sheriff. And don't worry, there are fifty men in here, including myself, who will swear you shot in self-defense. Excuse me, be back in a minute. Those carcasses are blocking the door. Somebody might fall over 'em and get hurt if we don't move 'em."

"Mr. Yates is nice, but I'm afraid he is a mite salty, as the boys would say," Jerry remarked pensively.

Slade purposely refrained from examining the bodies until the sheriff arrived, which he did in short order. He glanced at the corpses, now laid out in an orderly row, and came straight to the table.

"Didn't I tell you they were after you?" he said accusingly to Slade.

"Well, I had Jerry with me this time, too," the Ranger replied smilingly.

"I'm afraid I wasn't much help this time," Jerry interpolated.

"Oh, yes you were," he differed. "You're a good luck piece." Jerry giggled.

"Trouble! trouble! trouble!" groaned the sheriff. "Wherever you show up there's trouble! Sometimes I wish I'd never seen you."

"Six feet and a little more of nice trouble," Jerry observed blithely.

"Maybe for you, but not for me," Carter grumbled. "I could stand a mite of peace and quiet for a change. Guns started blazing soon as he hit town, and they'll keep on blazing till he leaves."

"At the rate he's going, there won't be any, of the wrong sort, left to blaze," Jerry replied dryly.

"You may have something there," the sheriff admitted. "Come on, Walt, and let's look the hellions over."

"Ornery looking devils," he commented a few minutes later. "Some of the Sosna bunch, of course."

"Reasonable to believe so," Slade agreed.

The bodies revealed nothing of significance aside from a good deal of money, which the sheriff pocketed.

"Will help pay for planting 'em," he observed. "Come on, let's go back to the table and get a drink. Yates will have them packed to the office.

"I'll ride out tomorrow and pick up the other three," he added as they sat down. "We'll hold an inquest on the collection day after tomorrow. Reckon you'd better be here, Walt."

"Me, too," Jerry said. "I was sort of mixed up in it."

"Yes, guess so," the sheriff agreed.

"Will give me another night in town," she whispered to Slade. To the sheriff—

"We'll have to ride back to the ranch in the morning or Uncle Keith will worry, but we'll be here day after tomorrow on time for the inquest."

"Okay," Carter nodded.

"And now I think we had better be going," Slade said. "It's past midnight and you've had a rather busy day."

"Keep your eyes skun," the sheriff warned.

Slade did walk warily until they reached the better lighted streets, although he did not really expect further trouble. He knew that the two men who started the row at the bar had slid out during the excitement. Very likely, however, their nerves had been pretty well shaken by the failure of their companions and would probably steer clear of him.

They reached the hotel lobby without incident, where they found the old desk clerk slumped back in his chair, his eyes closed, his mouth slightly open.

"He's sound asleep, or says he is," Jerry whispered. She glanced at the stairs, glanced at Slade.

SIXTEEN

WHEN SLADE DESCENDED from his little room over the stalls, about midmorning, old Clint, the keeper snorted.

"Don't you young fellers ever really sleep?" he complained. "I heard you come in, and it was already getting light."

"Guess I've got some owl blood and don't need much sleep," Slade replied cheerfully.

After bathing and shaving he went to look up Jerry and take her to breakfast, if she hadn't already eaten. He found her sitting in the hotel lobby.

"Finished my shopping," she announced, holding up two very small bundles.

"Is that all you rode to town for?" he asked.

"Not altogether," she replied. "We had a nice ride, didn't we? Lots of excitement and—everything."

"We certainly did," he agreed heartily. "Had breakfast?"

"No, I waited to eat with you," she replied. "Now I'm starving. First, though, I'm going to buy you that new rainshed, as you call it, as I said I would last night. Shut up! don't argue with me. I know what I'm doing. Do you want me to throw a tantrum?"

Slade gave up, and when they left a nearby shop he was wearing the new rainshed.

They had breakfast at the Trail End, which was close by, then headed back to the spread over the sun-golden prairie. Slade was silent as they rode, for he was occupied with his thoughts. Looked like the same old story. With the help of others, he was thinning out Sosna's bunch; but Sosna still eluded him, which meant that his chore was far from finished.

Just the same, the presentiment that this was showdown persisted. He felt that here the long tally of the years was drawing to a close. He hoped so, for he was heartily weary of the long pursuit of the elusive outlaw leader. Yes, let the blasted chase end, one way or another.

Jerry was also silent. Suddenly, however, she turned in her saddle to face him.

"Walt," she said, "just what are you? You're no chuck-line-riding cowhand. Don't try to fool me into thinking you are. Really, what are you?"

"You've heard of *El Halcón's* reputation, haven't you?" he countered, smilingly.

"Oh, the devil!" she exploded. "That nonsense! Please, I think you should tell me."

"Yes, I think I should," he agreed. He slipped the Ranger star from its pocket and handed it to her.

She studied it for a moment, her expressive eyes darkening, then passed it back to him.

"I see," she said slowly. "And I'm beginning to understand, now . . . 'The dust of gypsy feet'!"

"Sooner or later the dust must settle," he reminded her.

"Yes," she replied moodily, "unless it's kicked up again by the ever-moving feet. Oh, well!"

As was habitual with him, Slade rode warily. However, he was not at all apprehensive. Here on the open prairie nobody would take him unawares, and with his Winchester ready to hand, nobody could approach to within shooting range.

Jerry soon shook off her somber mood and chattered gaily as they jogged along at a good pace.

"Just wait until Uncle Keith hears of our adventures!" she said.

"Perhaps he'll forbid you to ride with me again," Slade suggested.

"Not him," she answered confidently. "He and Dad were both always getting mixed up in something when they were young; he'll understand. Besides, I'm past twenty-one and nobody can give me orders."

"Nobody?"

"Well, hardly anybody," she modified her statement, with a smile and a dimple.

"Just the same," he conceded, "it seems to me that ever since I met you I've been doing just whatever you wanted me to do, even against my better judgment."

"Oh, a woman has her ways of getting things done she

wants done," Jerry replied airily. "And there are certain arguments a man finds hard to resist."

"Definitely!" he agreed, with emphasis.

It was just getting dark when they reached the ranchhouse. Old Keith was standing in the door. He whooped for a wrangler to care for the horses.

"Come on and eat, and tell me what you have been getting into," he said.

Jerry told him, in a rush of words. Old Keith swore explosively and without reserve.

"Sure wish I'd been with you," he growled. "Would have give me a heap of pleasure to line sights with the hellions. So you can cut a notch on your gun stock, eh, chick? Your dad could have cut eight or nine on his.

"Was a wild and wooly section back in those days, a lot wilder and woolier than it is now," he said to Slade. "We hadn't only cow thieves and such varmints to deal with but the Comanches and the Kiowas, too. They were bad. Never could tell when you might hear the war screech and find the roof on fire over your head. But we made out and finally packed most of 'em off to the reservations and sorta tamed the rest. Not bad fellers now, most of 'em. Could hardly blame them for not taking kind to the land being settled and the buffaloes slaughtered off. The buffaloes were everything to the Injuns. Well, the world moves, and there's no stopping it. Let's eat."

The following morning, Slade and Jerry again set out for Amarillo, to attend the inquest. They kept to the prairie trail and reached the Cowboy Capital without untoward incident.

The inquest was brief, the coroner's jury verdict terse and to the point. Slade was again commended for doing a good chore and the hope expressed he would keep it up. Jerry also came in for congratulations. And the sheriff was at least not scolded. After which everybody repaired to the Trail End for a drink and something to eat.

"This place is cozy and comfortable, and Mr. Sanders with his funny eyes is nice, but I like the Washout better," Jerry whispered to Slade. "Here I feel I have to be on my good behavior. I'm afraid to cross my legs for fear I'll shock somebody. Shut up! Don't you say it!"

Slade contented himself with smiling, and changed the subject.

98

"Okay," he said, "I'll take you to the Washout for dinner tonight; we'll go late."

Her eyes grew thoughtful. "I would like to go there, but, dear, isn't it unsafe for you? Perhaps we'd better stay away from the lake front, where it seems anything is liable to happen."

Slade shrugged his shoulders. "Things can happen anywhere," he replied. "I don't think the lake front has any monopoly on what might happen. But if you prefer not to take the risk—"

"That'll be enough of that kind of talk," she snapped, "I'm ready to take any sort of a risk, with you. I think I've proven that, definitely. And I don't scare easily, Mr. Slade!"

"Okay, Miss Norman," he chuckled. "We'll go where you'll feel free to—"

She reached across the table and put one small hand firmly over his mouth.

"The only way I can shut you up," she declared. "Thank goodness, here comes our food; that should keep you speechless for a while."

El Halcón acquiesced with a meekness that would have surprised most people who knew him. But not without reason. Not only was he very fond of her, but he recognized the shrewdness of the brain beneath the curly dark hair. Her judgment was good, her reactions swift, and she was capable of summing up a situation with speed. Her next remark substantiated his opinion.

"Yes," she said, "I think that often it is best to go to meet trouble rather than waiting for it to come to one. That way one has the advantage. Just as you did in the Valley, and the other night in the Washout. The unexpectedness of your actions threw those killers off balance."

"You have the right notion," he replied. "Seldom anything is gained by running."

"Unless you have the faster horse, which wasn't the case the other day," she said. "Let's eat."

A little later she further confirmed his judgment. "Walt," she said, "as Uncle Keith would say, your man Sosna took something of a larruping from the XT, in one way or another. Don't you think he might possibly seek to retaliate?"

Slade nodded vigorous assent. "That's one of the reasons I tentatively agreed to sign up with the XT," he replied.

99

"And another reason?"

"A glance in the back bar mirror will adequately answer that question," he smiled.

"That was nicely put, but as the old-time melodrama would have it, all men are gay deceivers," she laughed.

"I resent the implication," he protested. "Everything I've told you is gospel truth."

"Better and better, or worse and worse," she said, with a giggle. "Keep on and you'll have me believing it. Now soon as we finish eating I'm really going to do some shopping. I'll have the saddle pouches stuffed when we ride tomorrow. Meet you in the hotel lobby right after dark. How's that for bowing to the sacred proprieties?"

"The day clerk stays awake," he remarked, with apparent irrelevance.

Jerry blushed.

SEVENTEEN

AS HE WANDERED about the town, killing time till dark, Slade pondered Jerry Norman's shrewd surmise that Sosna might seek to even up the score with the XT. He had done such things before. Slade recalled the blazing ranchhouse of a cowman who had opposed the outlaw leader, from which he, Slade, had rescued the owner before cremation ensued and had collected a few scorches himself in the process.

Yes, Sosna might well strike at the XT spread. He must know by now that the death of four of his followers was chalked up against Keith Norman's outfit. And Sosna wouldn't forget. Perhaps it would be possible to set a trap for the vengeful devil.

But it would have to be something original and out of the ordinary. None of the time-honored expedients like a herd which would appear made to order for widelooping. That wouldn't work against Veck Sosna. Well, he'd give the matter thought and perhaps be able to formulate a plan that would work.

With which in view, he resolved to pay Sheriff Carter a visit and proceeded to do so.

He found that official ensconced behind his desk, smoking the pipe of peace and relaxation. Carter nodded and gestured to a chair.

Rolling a cigarette, Slade sat down and unburdened his mind.

"If we could just figure something that would attract the hellion," he summed up.

"Uh-huh, if," grunted Carter. "It's a darn big if. Right now I'm hanged if I can think of anything. He'd hardly be induced to make another try for the Tascosa stage. Nor for the railroad train, I'd say. Right now they're loaded with railroad police, and Sosna must know it."

"I'm afraid you're right on both counts," Slade agreed morosely. "Well, if I can't inveigle *amigo* Sosna to come looking for me, I'll have to go looking for him. Which is what I propose to do."

"Seems to me he's been looking for you quite frequently of late," the sheriff commented dryly.

"He's sent others looking for me," Slade corrected. "So far I've had but one glimpse of him as he skalleyhooted into the brush. Well, maybe I'll get a break."

"Or make one, as you usually do," said Carter.

"I hope you're right," Slade replied. He glanced at the darkening window and stood up.

"Now I'm going looking for something more pleasant," he announced.

"What's that?"

"Jerry Norman."

"You'd do well to stick by Jerry," Carter advised. "She's all wool and a yard wide."

"I fear she wouldn't feel complimented, but I get what you mean," Slade chuckled. "Be seeing you."

He had no difficulty finding Jerry. She was sitting in the hotel lobby, waiting for him. He dropped into a chair beside her and rolled another cigarette.

"All set for the Washout?" he asked.

"I am," she replied. "And, as usual, I'm hungry. Have your smoke and then we'll go. Don't rush, now, I'm not that

101

hungry, and I like to watch you smoke, even though then you do seem a million miles away from me. Who is she?"

"She ain't," was the ungrammatical response.

"I almost wish she was," Jerry sighed. "I'd take my chance against competition. When you're preoccupied like that I know you're thinking up some way to get into trouble."

Slade laughed and pinched out his cigarette butt. "Don't bother your pretty head about it, I'll make out," he replied. "Come on, let's go eat."

They found the Washout busy, as usual. Thankful Yates escorted them to their table, from which there was a good view of the swinging doors.

"I hope nothing happens tonight," Jerry said after a waiter took their order. "I'm getting to be like Sheriff Carter; I can stand a little peace and quiet for a while."

Jerry had her wish gratified. The Washout was gay and boisterous, but harmless. The night passed without incident. But Slade experienced an uneasy premonition that it was the calm before the storm.

He was right.

The following morning, they rode for the spread. When, some miles out of town, they reached a point where the trail forked. Slade slowed the pace a little, his gaze following the right fork which, he knew, led across the Canadian to Tascosa on the north bank of the river.

"I think I'll take a little ride over there before I sign up with you," he remarked. Jerry sighed.

"Really, there's no sense in your signing up," she said. "You won't stay, of course. Just remain our guest for as long as you wish."

"I wouldn't want to wear my welcome out," he protested.

"Will you please stop annoying me with such *praatjies!*" she retorted.

"Praatjies?"

"That's what Dutch Herman, who keeps the harness shop in Amarillo, calls idle chatter. Somehow it seems to fit."

"It does," Slade conceded, with a chuckle. "Okay, I'll be good."

"Don't strain yourself, but it really might be worth a trial," she replied tartly. Slade moved his horse a little closer to hers.

"That's better," she said, when her lips were free for speaking.

With harmony again established, they rode on, reaching the XT ranchhouse in due time without anything happening.

That night there was a poker game in the bunkhouse and Slade was invited to sit in. Jerry made a moue at him when he accepted but did not complain vocally.

Slade liked poker; especially as it always gave him an opportunity to study human nature, bringing out as it did certain attributes that ordinarily were concealed from view.

For instance, normally gay and boisterous Joyce Echols was a conservative player, studying the cards carefully, estimating the odds, the element of chance, endeavoring to balance the one against the other. While quiet old Cale Fenton was a plunger, playing recklessly, following his hunches, drawing successfully to an inside straight with only two cards left in the deck with which to fill it.

With the result that when the game finally broke up, a little past midnight, Echols was a loser, Fenton a winner. Slade managed to break about even, which was what he wished to do. Saying goodnight to the boys, he left the bunkhouse and headed for the ranchhouse and bed.

But before he reached the building, he slowed his pace, came to a halt. He was not sleepy, and he was restless, with an uneasiness of mind he was at a loss to account for. A presentiment of evil hung over him like a faint miasma, indefinable, misty-visioned but very real. He had felt it before and almost always it had been a precursor of some untoward happening. Rolling and lighting a cigarette, he strolled to the far edge of the grove, leaned against a convenient tree and gazed eastward across the shadowy prairie.

It was a still night, with not a breath of wind. There was no moon and the stars were veiled by a thin fleece of cloud through which they filtered a dim light that caused objects to assume an unreal grotesqueness. Such a night as might well be chosen by disembodied specters and elementals and goblins damned to hold high revel and raise blasphemous incantations to the Lord of Ill.

Slade felt that no doubt his mental uneasiness was but a product of the eerie night and tried to banish it as a figment of over-active imagination.

Without success; it persisted, seemed to grow stronger. He

103

muttered disgustedly under his breath and swept the prairie with his gaze.

Suddenly he stiffened, every sense at hair-trigger alertness. Out there on the shadowy expanse, movement had birthed, a drift of shadows amid the shadows. And as he watched, tensely, the shadows took concrete form, resolved to horsemen riding at a slow and deliberate pace. Two horsemen sitting their mounts close together, drawing nearer and nearer.

About a hundred yards from the ranchhouse was a couple of tufts of low growth. A few more minutes and the shadowy horsemen merged with the deeper shadow cast by the thickets and vanished from his sight.

Slade's eyes never left the dark bristle. He breathed deeply a moment later when from the shadow crept two dimly seen figures, crouching low as if to avoid detection. The riders had dismounted and were approaching the ranchhouse on foot. If they followed their present course they would reach it a dozen yards or so from the silent watcher.

What the devil were they up to? Slade didn't know, but abruptly he recalled a ranchhouse wrapped in flame of incendiary origin. That might be it—their intention to fire the building. And there had been no rain for an extended period; everything was dry as tinder. Let a blaze get anything like a start and it would be almost impossible to put out. His presentiment of evil abruptly lost its vagueness and became a grim fact.

Keeping in the deeper shadow cast by the trees, he glided forward a few paces, estimating the distance. Now the creeping pair were not more than a score of yards from the south wall of the ranchhouse, their approach slower, even more stealthy. He drew both guns. His voice rang out—

"Elevate! You're covered!"

The pair whirled at the sound of his voice. Slade's keen eyes caught the gleam of metal jutting toward him as the pair ducked and weaved. He pulled both triggers, was rewarded by a yelp of pain echoing the reports that rang out like thunder in the great stillness. Answering slugs whined past, but he was still in the shadow and it was blind shooting for the two night prowlers who were backing away from him as they fired.

Taking deliberate aim, Slade fired again, left and right. *And blew up the world!*

104

EIGHTEEN

At least it seemed that way. There was a blinding flash, a terrific roar. Slade was knocked heels over head by the concussion. Prone on the ground, half stunned, blinded, his ears ringing like chiming bells, he vaguely sensed a tinkle and clatter of falling glass.

Not much wonder, though. Every window on that side of the ranchhouse was shattered, the frames of the nearest twisted and splintered by the force of the explosion.

Dizzy, floundering, Slade groped for and found his fallen guns. Then, still dazed, he managed to struggle to his feet and stand weaving, his guns mechanically pointing toward the smoking crater hollowed out in the ground a score of paces from the house. Yells and curses were splitting the night air. The screams of frightened horses in the barn and the nearby horse corral added to the ungodly tumult.

From the bunkhouse, which also had more than one broken window, bellowed the cowboys in all stages of undress. A light flashed on in the ranchhouse. The front door banged open and Jerry appeared in a flowered robe, old Keith in a long nightshirt.

"What the blankety-blank-blank happened?" he bawled. I thought the roof fell in!"

Albeit still somewhat shaken, Slade had recovered his composure.

"If those hellions had managed to plant the dynamite under the house like they planned to do, it very nearly would have," he replied, gesturing with one gun toward the deep and wide hole which still smoked.

"What happened—why'd it go off?" Norman demanded, looking dazed.

"I guess one of my slugs hit the bundle and set it off," Slade answered.

Jerry had slipped down the steps and was clinging to him. "Are you all right?" she asked anxiously.

"Perfectly," he reassured her, holstering his guns and patting her shoulder. "I wasn't close enough to get the full effect of the blast, and dynamite tends to blow down rather than up. Sort of addled my thought processes for a moment, but nothing more."

"How'd you catch on to what they were up to?" Norman asked.

"I didn't, but figured they were up to no good," Slade replied. "I had a notion they planned to set the house afire, perhaps. I happened to be standing at the edge of the grove and saw them coming. When I called to them to reach for the sky, they went for their irons and I had to shoot. No, I didn't think of dynamite, but I should have. Dynamite is a Sosna specialty."

Old Keith shook his head in bewilderment. "The snake-blooded varmint!" he rumbled. "I wouldn't have believed there was a man alive who would do such a thing!" Slade repeated something he had said once before,

"Veck Sosna isn't a man—he's a devil!"

"I believe it," growled Norman. Jerry shuddered and pressed closer to Slade.

The cowhands, while listening to Slade explain what happened, had gathered around the hole. Suddenly a voice shouted,

"Hey! here's an arm!"

"And here's a head, or what's left of it," somebody else whooped.

Slade took Jerry's arm and urged her up the steps and into the ranchhouse.

"There are things out here not good to look upon," he said gently.

Her face was pale, her eyes great dark pools of shadow, but she smiled wanly.

"I'm going out to the kitchen and make some coffee," she said. "I hear Pedro bumbling around out there and swearing in half a dozen different languages; he doesn't like to have his rest disturbed."

"Watch out for broken glass on the floor," Slade cautioned. "I'll be with you shortly; some coffee wouldn't go bad."

Outside, lanterns had been procured from the bunkhouse

and the barn, by the light of which the cowboys were conducting a systematic search of the yard. Joyce Echols approached Slade. He looked as if he wasn't feeling too good in the pit of his stomach."

"It's a mess," he said. "There are chunks of meat scattered all over. We're trying to get 'em piled in one heap, but I'm scared we can't assemble the parts. Don't know what belongs to who."

"Dynamite usually does a pretty fair job of disassembling, especially at close range," Slade agreed. "Cover the heap with tarps or blankets and we'll send for Johnny Davenport and turn 'em over to him."

"Guess we can get enough together to hold an inquest on," Echols replied cheerfully as he puffed hard on a cigarette he had rolled, and was apparently feeling better. "Scairt we'll have to use a blotter to get 'em all," he added with grisly humor. "But we're sure all going to need a bath when this chore is over."

Leaving the cowboys to do the mopping up, Slade returned to the house. He found old Keith, who had thrown on some clothes, sitting in a chair smoking. The lines in his big face seemed deeper.

"So it was a try at evening up the score, eh?" he remarked heavily. "Jerry mentioned that she thought there might be a chance they'd try something."

"Yes, I was afraid of something of the sort," Slade admitted. "Veck Sosna never forgets, and he never forgives. Well, his luck didn't hold overly well this time."

"Uh-huh, thanks to your foresight and courage," said Norman. "Guess you didn't just *happen* to be out there and see those hellions."

"Rather, it was just that I didn't happen to be sleepy," Slade corrected him. "I was walking around trying to get drowsy when I had the luck to spot them riding this way."

Old Keith grunted, and didn't appear much impressed.

"Coffee's on the table," Jerry called from the kitchen. "And Pedro's making his big boiler full to take out to the boys when they're ready for it. Then I think everybody should go to bed and try and get an hour or two of sleep before daylight."

Old Keith nodded agreement. "And tomorrow, today, rather, we'll have a chore of repair work to do," he said.

107

"Wouldn't be surprised if the wall's ready to tumble down, to say nothing of all those windows blowed to smithereens. Well, thanks to Slade, things turned out a heap better than they might have done. If that dynamite had cut loose under the house, right now the chances are we'd be taking up ourselves with a blotter."

"A somewhat difficult procedure, but I think I gather what you mean," Jerry observed from the doorway. "Come and get it!"

They drank the coffee, then everybody tumbled into bed, pretty well exhausted by the wild night.

First, Slade walked to the door and gazed for a moment at the grim, blanket-covered mound beside the gaping hole. He drew a deep breath of thankfulness that he had followed what amounted to a hunch and had rendered abortive the devilish scheme to get even Sosna had evolved. Had the bundle of dynamite been exploded under the building, it was quite likely that none of the occupants would have survived and at the very best would have suffered severe injury.

Well, he had scored a point against the Comanchero leader with the odds against him. Perhaps Sosna's unbelievable luck was running out. Slade believed it was. He went upstairs with his mind more at ease than it had been for some time.

Slade was awakened about mid-morning by a prodigious hammering and sawing and considerable whole-hearted profanity. Evidently the hands were busy at the repair job. He listened for a little while, then arose, made ready for breakfast and descended to the living room, where he found Jerry.

"All right?" she asked. "I wouldn't let them start their racket until I was sure you'd gotten some rest. You were so very, very tired."

"Well, it was a hard night, everything considered," he replied, the devils of laughter in the back of his eyes leaping to the front. Jerry smiled and dimpled and let it go at that.

"Come on," she said, jumping to her feet. "Your breakfast is waiting for you; I'll have coffee with you."

After eating, Slade went out to inspect the damage done by the explosion. After a careful examination, he decided the building wall had suffered only trivial effects and required no attention save a bit of a paint job. The shattered windows were being properly taken care of.

"We sent for the sheriff," Bolivar, the range boss, told him. "He'd oughta get here in an hour or two. Hope he shows up soon; we can do without that." He gestured to the blanket-covered mound as he spoke.

"We found a few more hunks when we got up and it was light," he added. "Guess everything's cleaned up now, except for filling that hole in the ground. Sensible thing to do would be to dump 'em in that and shovel dirt over 'em, but Miss Jerry seems to want to get 'em off the place. Reckon she don't want to be reminded of what would have happened if it wasn't for you. A fine chore, féller, a raunchin' fine chore."

Satisfied that everything was progressing satisfactorily, Slade returned to the ranchhouse. A little later old Keith dropped in from his own tour of inspection.

"Lucky we had a cutter and a bit of glass left over from when we enlarged the bunkhouse windows," he said. "If we need more we'll get it from Amarillo. Figure we've got enough to patch up most of the holes. By the way, the boys rooted out the horses those hellions rode. Good critters; they're in the barn lining their bellies. Guess we got a right to keep 'em."

"You certainly have," Slade agreed. "Will sort of make up for the damage done."

"Would have been a heck of a sight more if you hadn't stopped the sidewinders when you did," Norman growled. "Well, they sure got what was coming to 'em in a hurry. That's what you call going to hell in a basket, I reckon, and not just talk. The blankety-blank-blanks!"

"Watch your language, Uncle Keith, you'll shock Walt," Jerry warned. "Not me, I'm used to it."

An hour later Sheriff Davenport arrived. "Jake told us what happened, so we brought a passel of burlap sacks and a shovel in the wagon. Guess we'll need 'em, from what he said."

"And when you get 'em loaded into the wagon, drive it down beyond the horse corral for the night," said Norman. "They must be startin' to get ripe in the sun."

Jerry shuddered. "Oh, for heaven's sake, don't joke about it," she protested. "It was terrible."

"Could have been worse, could have been worse," old Keith said cheerfully. "*We* might have been on the receivin' end. We would have, I reckon, if it wasn't for Walt."

"The whole section's on the prod against Sosna and his

109

hellions," observed Davenport. "Folks have been jumpin' on me with all four feet. I've got a deputy and four specials setting out to comb the Valley this afternoon. A Mexican feller—'least he looked like a Mexican—came in and said he saw a jigger answering Sosna's description at a plaza over toward the New Mexico Line. I told the boys to snuk up on that plaza and keep a watch on it. If Sosna does happen to have a hangout there, they'd have a good chance to drop a loop on him."

El Halcón suddenly looked grave. "Over to the west, near the New Mexico line?" he repeated. "I think I recall that plaza. Couple of big sheep ranches a little farther west, aren't there? Used to be."

"That's right," replied Davenport. "They're still there."

Slade nodded, and did not comment further. A little later, however, after the sheriff had gone out to collect the remains of the dead outlaws, he abruptly stood up.

"I'm going to take a little ride," he told Jerry.

"May I go with you?" she asked, her eyes darkening.

"Not this time," he refused. The set of his face, and the look in his cold eyes she had learned to dread forbade her pressing the request.

"Please be careful," she begged.

"Don't worry," he answered, patting her shoulder. "I'll be okay." He strode out, leaving a badly worried girl behind.

NINETEEN

SLADE WASTED NO TIME getting the rig on Shadow. As he rode away from the ranchhouse, Sheriff Davenport straightened up from his grisly task and gazed after him.

"Now what's he up to?" he wondered to his deputy.

"I don't know," replied the deputy, "but I'll bet a hatful of pesos somebody is going to find out and not like the finding. Blazes! what a pair of eyes! Gave me the creeps."

Slade rode at a leisurely pace until he was out of sight of the ranchhouse, then he gradually speeded up. Shadow seemed to enjoy a chance to really stretch his legs, for he tossed his head, rolled his eyes and fairly poured his long body over the ground.

"Horse," Slade told him, "I don't know, but somehow what Johnny Davenport said had an off-color sound to me. I don't believe Sosna has a hangout in the west Valley. His stamping grounds have always been over to the east, where he can slide across the Oklahoma Line or take a straight shoot to the Cap Rock hills. And right now I've a notion he's in a raving temper and itching to kill at the first opportunity. He hasn't been having much luck of late and he doesn't like that. Killing a few folks would soothe his injured feelings. That's always been the way with him."

Shadow snorted cheerful agreement. Slade paused to roll and light a cigarette, then resumed:

"Yes, he must be in a killing mood right now. And those clumsy specials might very well amble into a trap. A fellow Johnny thought looked like a Mexican brought the word. Could be, but then again he could be one of Sosna's Comancheros. The Mexican sheepherders in the Valley are mighty close-mouthed when it comes to talking about Sosna and his doings, and for one to ride up to the sheriff's office with such information seems to me a bit out of line. So, horse, we're going to play a hunch. Could be that it'll pay off. Anyhow, it's a nice afternoon for a ride, and I figure we haven't anything to lose. I've no notion where to look for Sosna, so I believe it's a good idea to follow anything that looks at all like a lead. Well, we'll see."

The sun was walking down the western slant of the sky, but it still lacked some hours till dark. Slade estimated the probable speed of the riding specials and the distance they might be expected to cover. He believed he was well ahead of them. Which was what he wanted to be. He reasoned they would almost certainly follow the river trail, their objective the plaza of which Davenport spoke.

He knew that for some miles east of the plaza in question, the growth which flanked the trail was sparser than average, but with occasional dense thicket that would provide excellent cover for a lurking band. Glancing at the sun, he urged Shadow to hand out a bit more speed. The black horse responded and Slade did not ease him until they had covered several miles.

"Okay, feller, let the dust settle," he said. "Here's where we turn off."

With which he swerved the horse to the north and rode for the lip of the Valley now little more than a mile distant. On the edge of the great depression he pulled to a halt and for several minutes sat gazing eastward.

"Well, here goes," he said. "Maybe we're just headed for a fool's errand, but I'm still playing my hunch that we aren't. Down you go, feller, doesn't look tòo bad here."

Shadow had no difficulty negotiating the fairly steep slope and reached the Valley floor without incident. Slade again halted him and surveyed the surrounding terrain. Then he rode steadily for a couple of miles, threading his way through the chaparral, and still again halted. Now he was close to the trail, and here, nearer the Valley wall, the growth was thicker than along the track which ran not far from the river and steadily paralleling the stream.

Turning east, he rode slowly, scanning the eastward reaches with care. There were occasional rises from which he could catch a glimpse of the trail for some distance ahead. So far it lay lonely and deserted, with no indication of movement other than that of little animals or birds that nested in the bushes.

These last interested him most, for he looked upon them, from the personal viewpoint, as harbingers of goodwill. Time after time, their reactions had saved him from disaster. Walt Slade knew the forests as he knew the prairie and knew that the woods will be good to you if you give them the chance. Their dwellers could be faithful friends did one but study them and understand them.

So as he rode he kept close watch on his feathered *amigos*, confident that they would give him warning were something untoward concealed behind the leafy screens, studying every flight and settling, looking for indications of alarm or irritation.

But as he rode he began to grow uneasy, to be haunted by a fear that he might have underestimated the speed with which the small posse would travel and was in error as to where, in his judgment, the trap, if one were really contemplated, might be set. His own progress was slow, threading

112

his way through the brush, and he did not care to risk premature discovery by riding the trail.

The miles dragged back under Shadow's hoofs, and still each glimpse he had of the trail showed it deserted and peaceful. But it was an ominous sort of peace, the kind of a peace that broods under a lowering sky with lightning flickers on the distant horizon. Slade, sensitive to all impressions, felt his uneasiness increasing. He began mounting a low rise and for some little time he could not scan the trail. Finally he topped it and glanced ahead.

The trail ran at a somewhat lesser elevation and from where he sat his horse he could see for more than half a mile along a straight stretch tufted farther on by bristles of thicket. One, denser and broader than most, was perhaps five hundred yards from where the trail curved and vanished from sight. He himself was fully a thousand yards from the thicket.

It was a bird that warned him something was amiss. Over the thicket something danced and wheeled and darted. It was but a mere speck against the sky, but *El Halcón's* keen vision instantly recognized it to be an angry bluejay that doubtless had a nest in the thicket.

Now what could have set old fuss-and-feathers to acting up? A coyote it would pay no mind; coyotes didn't stalk bluejays. A snake on a limb near the next? Nope, it would peck the eyes out of the reptile if it approached too close. Something it didn't understand and feared was beneath the leafy screen. Slade's eyes narrowed, he glanced ahead, and uttered an exclamation.

Around the bend of the trail five horsemen had appeared, riding at a fair pace; they would pass within but a few yards of the thicket. And very quickly they would be within easy rifle range from anybody who might be holed up in the brush. And Slade was very much of the opinion that somebody was holed up there, and not just to enjoy the scenery. The little posse would be settin' quail for ambushing riflemen in a very few minutes.

In a flickering second of time the Ranger estimated the distance. He could not hope to reach the thicket in time to warn the approaching riders. Nevertheless his voice rang out.

"Trail, Shadow, trail!"

The great horse lunged forward, his flying hoofs spurning

113

the earth. In and out of the straggle of brush he weaved and swerved, never slackening his racing speed. The ominous thicket seemed to flow forward.

"But we can't make it!" his rider muttered. "Not in time. Only thing to do is try to create a diversion and warn those careless coots."

As he spoke, he slid his Winchester from the saddle boot, clamped the butt against his shoulder and sent a stream of lead hissing through the thicket.

The effect was instantaneous. The approaching horsemen jerked to a halt, still four hundred yards or so from the clump of growth, and sat staring in the direction of the blazing rifle. And from the growth bulged half a dozen men on foot. They could see Slade racing toward them on the slightly higher elevation. Flame flickered from their ranks. Bullets whined past the speeding horseman.

Leaning low in the saddle, Slade jammed fresh cartridges into the magazine of his rifle. He flung it to his shoulder, his cold eyes glanced along the sights.

It was long shooting from the back of a speeding horse, but just the same when the rifle spoke, one of the drygulchers flung up his arms and pitched to the ground. A slug fanned Slade's face, another ripped the sleeve of his shirt. Then as the Winchester roared, a second man reeled forward and fell.

But Slade knew he was on a spot. Now the four remaining outlaws had dropped to one knee and were taking deliberate aim. And men on foot had the advantage over a horseman. He set his teeth against the tearing impact of a well placed bullet. He had been so busy with the immediate chore that he had forgotten the sheriff's posse, but now he realized that more guns were banging. He glanced ahead, saw the five riders racing for the thicket, shooting as they came.

The drygulchers, caught between a deadly crossfire, leaped erect and darted back toward the thicket, but too late. Two went down, another reeled, staggered and plunged forward on his face. The last devil almost made it. In the very shadow of the brush he fell to lie motionless. There was no way of knowing whether it was *El Halcón*'s bullet or one fired by the posse that gave him his comeuppance.

Slade eased Shadow and rode to meet the specials, who were waving their hands and shouting to him. He waved back and continued at a steady pace.

One of the horsemen suddenly let out an astounded bellow. "Slade!" he whooped. "Where in blazes did you come from?" Slade recognized him to be Josh Klingman, the deputy who had accompanied Sheriff Davenport on his visit to the XT ranchhouse the day after the attempted widelooping.

"Howdy, Josh?" he called back. "I was coming looking for you fellows."

"Well, you sure found us at just the right time," answered Klingman. "If it hadn't been for you, right now us fellers would be coyote bait. In another minute those sidewinders would have mowed us down. How the blankety-blank-blank did they know *we* were coming this way?"

"They lured you into coming this way, with that phony story of Veck Sosna being holed up in the plaza over to the west," Slade replied as he reined in and began manufacturing a cigarette.

Klingman stared at him, shook his head. He glanced at the sprawled bodies of the outlaws, wet his suddenly dry lips with the tip of his tongue, and when he spoke his voice shook a little.

"Johnny swears you always do just the right thing," he said slowly. "From now on I figure to help him with his swearin'. And you figured it out that the yarn that Mexican feller brought Johnny was just so much sheep dip?"

"Well, it didn't sound just right to me," Slade conceded. "The Mexicans of the Valley are not in the habit of discussing Veck Sosna and his whereabouts. Certainly not with a law enforcement officer. That's a good way to bust up a dull day for the undertaker and they know it. Sosna is mad as Hades over the way things have been breaking for him of late and was out to even the score a mite. Killing off a few peace officers would make him feel better."

"Uh-huh, and if you hadn't happened along when you did, I've a notion tonight he'd have been feeling pretty darn good," one of the specials remarked dryly. "Much obliged, feller, we won't forget it. And you sure took a chance, riding right into rifle fire like that."

Slade smiled and deftly changed the subject. "Suppose we look them over and then locate their horses," he suggested. "I expect the best thing we can do is load the bodies onto the cayuses and head for Tascosa. Davenport will be there by the time we arrive; not long till dark."

"A good notion," agreed Klingman. "We'd figured to get to that blasted plaza over to the west after dark, hole up and watch on the chance that Sosna was there. Pres, see if you can find the horses while we give the carcasses a once-over."

The slain outlaws, Slade thought, were with one exception typical of the Comanchero brand. The exception was a scrawny individual with a crooked nose whose dark face seemed to indicate a mixture of Spanish and Indian blood. Josh Klingman peered at him and let out one of his bellows.

"That's the blankety-blanked horned toad who brought that yarn about Sosna to Johnny!" he swore. "Well, he's told his last blankety-blank lie, unless he aims to try one out on the Devil."

Slade nodded, not particularly surprised. "Slid out of town and hightailed to set the trap," he said. "Let's see what they have on them, nothing of any significance, the chances are."

He was right. The pockets of the dead men revealed only the usual trinkets carried by range riders, and a large sum of money. Klingman fingered the bills and glanced at Slade.

"Feller, if you can use this dinero, you've sure earned it," he said significantly. The others nodded agreement.

Slade smiled at them, and the devils of laughter in the back of the cold eyes turned somersaults to the front and suddenly were very warm and likeable devils.

"Thank you, boys," he said, "but I don't exactly need it and perhaps you fellows can put it to a better use. I'm going to see how Pres is making out with the horses."

"Fellers, there goes a real gent," observed Klingman as he began dividing the money into five equal piles. "There are folks what say *he's* the owlhoot, but I sort of got my doubts. I'm stringing along with Johnny Davenport, who 'lows no matter what else he is, he's a real hombre."

TWENTY

PRES HAD LOCATED the horses and was busy loosing them from the branches to which they were tethered when Slade joined him.

"Good looking cayuses, all right," he observed.

"Yes," Slade agreed. "Sosna is an excellent judge of horse flesh and always manages to tie onto first-class critters for himself and his men."

The bodies were roped to the saddles and the cavalcade got under way, Slade riding somewhat to the front and very much on the alert. He did not really expect any further trouble, but with the unpredictable Sosna it was best to take no chances. And stronger and stronger grew the presentiment that the final showdown between him and the outlaw leader was not far off.

It was a long and wearisome ride to Tascosa, for the awkwardly laden horses made the going slow, and the hour was close to midnight when they sighted the lights of the town on the north bank of the Canadian River. They clattered across the bridge and headed for the sheriff's office, very quickly picking up a following from the streets and the saloons.

"Tell you later," Klingman shouted answer to the questions volleyed at them. "Keep out, now, Johnny'll have a fit if you come bulging into the office."

They found Sheriff Davenport in the office, awaiting their possible arrival, and he was in anything but a good temper. Slade lingered outside a moment to look after Shadow.

"Well, s'pose you couldn't find him, eh?" he growled. "I expected it. Should have known better than to send boys to do a man's chore. What the devil's all that racket outside? Somebody having a wring?"

"Reckon not," Klingman replied. "Nope, we didn't find

him, but picked up a few souvenirs for you; got 'em outside. Come and look at them."

"Souvenirs!" snorted the sheriff. "You would waste your time rounding up doo-dads. All right, all right, I'll look at them."

As he reached the door, he spotted *El Halcón*'s tall form. "Slade!" he exclaimed. "Where the devil did you come from? How did—hey! what the blankety-blank—" His voice trailed off in a sputter as he stared at the grim burdens borne by the led horses.

"Come on back in and I'll tell you about it," said Klingman. "Don't worry about *them*—they'll keep. All right, you rum guzzlers, stay outside; I'll talk to you later."

In the office, the story came out with a rush, spiced by vivid profanity. The dumbfounded sheriff listened in silence, his mouth slightly open. When Klingman paused, he stood up and solemnly shook hands with Slade.

"You're the limit!" he growled. "You'll be the death of me yet. But thank God for you!"

"Amen," said Klingman, and the way he said it sounded like the conclusion of a prayer.

"And I never caught on," added Davenport. "That hellion's story about Sosna being holed up over around that plaza of sheep growers sounded like the real thing to me."

"He ain't telling any more stories," Klingman varied his former remark. "He'll be on ice tonight with the rest of 'em. Yep, we got him outside."

"And now," Slade said, "I crave some coffee and something to eat."

"Me, too," said Davenport. "Haven't had a bite since I ate at the XT ranchhouse. Remember Jenks' saloon, don't you, Walt? A good place to eat."

"Yes, I recall he put out a tasty surrounding," Slade agreed. "I'll take care of my horse and be with you."

"Take him around to McCormick's livery stable," directed the sheriff. "They'll remember you there. That's where I keep my cayuse. I'll wait here." He proceeded to give orders for the disposal of the bodies.

After making sure all of Shadow's wants were cared for, Slade returned to the office and found Davenport ready to amble. Together they repaired to the big and brightly lighted saloon and ordered everything in sight.

"Now I feel better and all set for anything," Davenport said, with a sigh, as he drained a final cup of steaming coffee. "How about you?"

"Fine as frog hair," Slade replied. "Beginning to get a mite sleepy, though."

"Guess you can get a room at the Exchange Hotel, right down the street from the livery stable, and it's okay," Davenport said.

"Yes," Slade agreed; "I've slept there. I think I'll round up my saddle pouches and head for a little ear pounding."

"Be holding an inquest over those varmints and the gunny sacks of meat I brought from the XT," the sheriff announced. "Some time in the afternoon—'round two or three o'clock, I reckon, so sleep as long as you want to."

Procuring his pouches from the livery stable, Slade registered for a room at the Exchange Hotel. However, he did not immediately lie down. After cleaning and oiling his rifle, he sat by the open window for a while smoking and listening to Tascosa's busy night life. Seemed the darn town never slept—bad as Amarillo.

He wondered just where was Sosna at the moment. His bunch must be pretty well thinned out and it was logical to believe he might be on a hunt for replacements, which he could conceivably find difficult to corral. Even the tough and ruthless Comancheros might be a bit reluctant to trust themselves to his leadership, in view of recent happenings. Aside from his successful raid on the express car, Sosna hadn't enjoyed much luck of late, his followers less, and even hardened owlhoots would look somewhat askance at a leader who dispatched his men on missions that proved to be rendezvous with death.

That a number of his men had died meant nothing, personally, to Sosna. His callous disregard for the sanctity of human life extended to his associates. To him they were but a means to an end, instruments for furthering his evil aims. And if he remained on the loose, sooner or later he would get together another following—he was a genius at that.

Meanwhile, something original and daring might be expected of him, something to restore confidence in his ability. Greed was the mainspring of the outlaw brand, and a leader who could keep his hellions' pockets well lined never lacked long for adherents.

119

Slade wracked his brains to fathom what the cunning devil might have in mind, and failed to come up with the answer. At least, however, he formulated a plan of action which he resolved to put into effect. Pinching out his cigarette, he went to bed.

Shortly before noon found him awake, well rested, and hungry. After washing up, he repaired to Jenks' saloon, where he put away a bountiful breakfast. Next he dropped in at the sheriff's office for a word with Johnny Davenport.

"Inquest at two o'clock," the peace officer announced. "Won't take long. Then what do you figure to do?"

"I'm riding to Amarillo," Slade replied. "Sort of following another hunch, as it were."

"Do you think Sosna might be there?" the sheriff asked curiously.

"Rather, that he might show up there," Slade said.

"Better watch your step, he or some of his hellions might be laying for you along the way," Davenport warned.

"I doubt it," Slade returned. "He's cunning and farsighted, but he's not omniscient, or at least so I believe, although at times I've wondered a mite as to that. No reason, so far as I can see, that he should suspect me of heading that way, even if he has already learned I'm here in Tascosa."

Just the same, Slade took no chances when he rode east a little later, and was thoroughly on the alert for the unexpected, the unexpected being Veck Sosna's specialty.

His first objective was old Estaban's cabin, where he received a warm welcome from the Mexican. And as they sat together over coffee and cigarettes, Estaban had news for him.

"Capitan," he said, "one who answered the description of him you seek rode past this morning. Tall, broad, a tiger-like man with eyes that seemed to burn. I saw him from inside my adobe, the door of which was shut, and was thankful that he did not see me."

"Sounds like Sosna, all right," Slade conceded. "He rode east?"

"That is right," replied Estaban. "He rode not fast."

After saying goodbye to Estaban and continuing on his way, Slade did some hard thinking. No doubt but the rider the Mexican described was Sosna. Which brought up a couple of questions that demanded answer and without delay.

120

Had Sosna, after learning that the man he regarded as his nemesis was in Tascosa, by some miraculous exercise of his devious thought processes concluded that he, Slade, would ride to Amarillo by way of the river trail and planned to wait for him somewhere along the way? Or had he decided that with Slade in Tascosa, the way was clear to him for a visit to the Cowboy Capital for some purpose of his own, possibly to recruit more followers? Slade believed the latter; but the former was not to be disregarded, for in some ways Veck Sosna was positively uncanny.

And his life might well hang on the answer to those questions.

But as the miles flowed past under Shadow's hoofs and nothing happened and the point where he would leave the ominous Valley for the open prairie drew near, his unease lessened. In fact, Sosna might not even have known he was in Tascosa. Also, he might plan to bypass Amarillo and proceed to the Cap Rock hills, where he would find a much less dubious sanctuary and be able to recruit a new following at his leisure.

Slade hoped not, for that would mean the wearisome and seemingly unending pursuit must start all over. If he could just find Sosna in Amarillo, the matter might be settled one way or another.

A little later, he turned south, climbed the Valley slope and reached the prairie trail, and rode on under the stars.

The lights of Amarillo came into view, golden sparks against the background of the night. Shadow, anticipating oats, quickened his pace. Soon they were clattering through the outskirts of the town.

Slade stabled his mount and headed for the Trail End, which was nearby, for something to eat. He thought he might probably find Sheriff Carter or Deputy Harley there, for the sheriff's office was dark.

However, neither peace officer was present, nor did they put in an appearance while he ate. Rolling and lighting a cigarette, he sat pondering his next move, arrived at a decision.

Leaving the Trail End, he began to systematically comb the town, with no results. Looked like his hunch wasn't a straight one. But the presentiment that close at hand was the final showdown persisted, grew stronger.

121

The lake front places, boisterous and rowdy, produced nothing of interest. As a last resort he entered the Washout, glancing quickly around. Present was the usual crowd of drinkers, gamblers and dancers, nothing more. Slade found a table from which he had a clear view of the door, sat down and ordered a drink, which he sipped morosely.

Suddenly the swinging doors opened and a man entered, a tall, broad, tiger-like man whose flashing black eyes swept the room in an all-embracing glance.

Walt Slade surged to his feet, took a stride forward, another. At long last, *El Halcón* and Veck Sosna stood face to face!

Two hands moved like a blur of light. Two guns blazed as one. Slade reeled slightly, steadied himself, fired again. Sosna also fired again. Slade scarcely felt the burn of the slug along his left arm, for his whole left side was a flame of pain. Again he steadied himself, and once more he shot, left and right, left and right. Veck Sosna raised himself on tiptoes and screamed, a horrible, rasping scream, the bell notes of his voice cracked and jangled. For an instant he stood erect, trying to lift the guns that dropped from his nerveless hands. Then he fell as falls a tall pine of the forest under the woodman's axe, slowly at first, then with a rush.

The saloon was a pandemonium of yells, screams and curses, but Veck Sosna did not hear them. He lay on his face, his life draining out through his shattered lungs.

The long tally of the years was ended!

Slade holstered his guns, his movements like to those of an automaton. A hush fell over the room as he took a halting step forward—another—another. Slowly he knelt beside Sosna's body. He reached out a fumbling hand, as if to raise the dead outlaw's head, and pitched forward.

The two motionless forms made a great cross on the barroom floor.

TWENTY-ONE

When Walt Slade recovered consciousness he was lying on a bed in a bright and airy room. He wondered vaguely where it was and how he got there. The problem was perplexing, endeavoring to solve it exhausting. Didn't really matter, anyhow. He felt curiously content to be right where he was.

He moved slightly and a twinge of pain shot through his left side. What the devil!

The twinge served to banish some of the cobwebs from his brain and recollection swept over him. Veck Sosna! Veck Sosna lying on the saloon floor! Well, Sosna would stay dead this time. He dimly recalled kneeling beside his body to make sure, and experienced a mild satisfaction.

Gradually he became aware of a sound of low voices somewhere near. One was deep and rumbling, the other soft and distinctly feminine. Who could it be? The feminine one reminded him of something. Oh, yes, it was very like Jerry Norman's voice. Couldn't be Jerry's, however. She was at the XT ranchhouse, while he must be in Amarillo. She wouldn't have had time to get here since last night, even if she heard of the gun fight in the Washout. Perhaps if he turned his head he might be able to see who it was. It required some thought to make up his mind to do so. Finally he did, and wondered why it entailed such effort. There was a glad little cry—

"Doctor! he's coming out of it!"

Another moment and he looked up into a face, a face that seemed all great tear-misted eyes. Absently he noted that the tears were running down her cheeks.

It was Jerry, all right, but how the devil did she get here? That was a question that required an answer; he groped to find it.

Suddenly Jerry's piquant little face changed, became wrinkled and hairy. Now *that* wasn't as it should be! Fingers clamped on his wrist, gently but persistently.

"Yep, he's come out of it and he'll be okay," said the rumbling voice.

His mind cleared still more. The hairy face belonged to old Doc Beard. Now he could see Jerry hovering in the background. He smiled at her, a trifle wanly, and gave his attention to Doc, who was speaking.

"How you feel?" he asked.

"Just fine," Slade replied, and wondered why his own voice sounded so weak.

"Good!" said the physician. "You'll be okay, but if that slug that went through your left side below the ribs had been an inch farther to the right, you wouldn't be here."

Slade's mind had cleared until he was his normal self, mentally, at least. He gazed at both of them for a moment.

"And I have a feeling," he said slowly, "that if it wasn't for you two, I wouldn't be here."

"Could be," Doc conceded cheerfully. "Anyhow, she sure has looked after you, hasn't left you a minute since she got here early yesterday."

"Yesterday? Why it was last night I had the rukus with Sosna!"

Doc laughed. "That was three nights ago," he replied. "Guess you were sorta tired and needed a lot of sleep; anyhow, you got it." He turned to Jerry.

"Okay," he told her. "He'll be up and about in a couple more days; figure he'll be able to ride the last of the week, if nothing goes wrong. All right, you can come over here with him, if you wish. I'll be back in a few minutes."

Jerry knelt beside the bed and laid her cheek against his hand.

"You looked so deathly, with your eyes closed and breathing heavily when I got here yesterday morning," she murmured, her voice quivering. "But Doctor Beard said it was more exhaustion, shock and a terrific nervous letdown rather than your wound that prostrated you. Joyce Echols was in town that night and brought the word of what had happened. I got here just as quickly as I could."

"And I wouldn't be surprised if it was just in time," he replied. "I've a strong notion that it was you who pulled me out of it; I believe I felt your presence."

124

"I hope so," she said, with a wan smile. "Makes me feel good to hear you say it, anyhow." She laid her cheek back on his hand, the big dark eyes closed. When old Doc returned a few minutes later, he chuckled.

"Sound asleep, and no wonder," he said. Picking her up in his strong old arms, he carried her to another room.

"I covered her up and that'll hold her for the next seven or eight hours," he remarked. "Brian Carter and Hartley and Keith Norman will be here shortly; they've been waiting for the word that you've got your senses back."

"Doc," Slade said, "something I want to ask you. Sosna was really dead, wasn't he?"

"Well, if he wasn't, a jigger with a shovel played a mighty mean joke on him up at Boot Hill," Doc returned dryly. Slade sighed with satisfaction.

"And that's over with, thanks to the Powers that be," he said. "This time I guess I can be sure."

Thanks to rugged health and clean living, Slade's recovery was swift. Four days later, Doc Beard agreed that he would be able to ride to the XT spread.

"But no shenanigans," he warned. "You're coming along fine, but you're not clean out of the woods yet. You know, there is such a thing as a relapse, which can be serious for even a strong man. Make him be good, Jerry."

"I will," she promised firmly.

Before leaving town, Slade had a few words with Sheriff Carter.

"No, I don't know for sure whether Sosna came looking for me or just happened into the Washout by chance," he replied to the sheriff's question.

"I rather think he did," Carter said. "Well, he found you, and I wouldn't be surprised if right now he's telling the Devil an angry yarn about you. They should get along together fine. I sure feel relieved. Be seeing you."

A little later, Slade and Jerry Norman rode out of Amarillo together. For some time they rode without speaking, slowly, charmed to silence by the beauty of the sun-drenched rangeland. Finally she broke the silence.

"Anyhow, I'll have you for a couple more weeks," she said. "The doctor insists that you do no extensive riding for at least that time. Then I suppose you'll be leaving."

"Yes," he answered. "I'll have to be getting back to the

Post to see what next Captain Jim has lined up for me. Right now I feel I've earned what I'm looking forward to as a very pleasant vacation."

Jerry smiled and dimpled. "I'll try to make it so," she said softly.

"You will, no doubt as to that," he declared with a heartiness that caused her to blush. They laughed together.

But she sighed as she gazed up at his sternly handsome face. " 'Dust of gypsy feet'!" she murmured to herself.

For already his steady eyes seemed to look afar, to where duty called and danger and new adventure beckoned.

THE END

Bradford Scott was a pseudonym for **Leslie Scott** who was born in Lewisburg, West Virginia. During the Great War, he joined the French Foreign Legion and spent four years in the trenches. In the 1920s he worked as a mining engineer and bridge builder in the western American states and in China before settling in New York. A bar-room discussion in 1934 with Leo Margulies, who was managing editor for Standard Magazines, prompted Scott to try writing fiction. He went on to create two of the most notable series characters in Western pulp magazines. In 1936, Standard Magazines launched, and in *Texas Rangers*, Scott under the house name of **Jackson Cole** created Jim Hatfield, Texas Ranger, a character whose popularity was so great with readers that this magazine featuring his adventures lasted until 1958. When others eventually began contributing Jim Hatfield stories, Scott created another Texas Ranger hero, Walt Slade, better known as *El Halcon*, the Hawk, whose exploits were regularly featured in *Thrilling Western*. In the 1950s Scott moved quickly into writing book-length adventures about both Jim Hatfield and Walt Slade in long series of original paperback Westerns. At the same time, however, Scott was also doing some of his best work in hardcover Westerns published by Arcadia House; thoughtful, well-constructed stories, with engaging characters and authentic settings and situations. Among the best of these, surely, are *Silver City* (1953), *Longhorn Empire* (1954), *The Trail Builders* (1956), and *Blood on the Rio Grande* (1959). In these hardcover Westerns, many of which have never been reprinted, Scott proved himself highly capable of writing traditional Western stories with characters who have sufficient depth to change in the course of the narrative and with a degree of authenticity and historical accuracy absent from many of his series stories.